Follow me:

Facebook: Smokey Moment Books

Twitter: Smokeymomentbooks

Instagram: Smokeymomentbooks

Acknowledgments

Dedicated to all the readers who love a good book that keeps you guessing, laughing, cursing, crying and all caught up in your emotions. A good book is powerful. You get to escape and use your own imagination to fill in the blanks. You get to travel all around the globe. Sometimes even to another planet. Possibly discover a new species. A good love story will have you daydreaming and fantasizing about what is and what could be. Or it could have you shaking your head in disbelief while you watch the *train wreck* of a life unfold. And then you hope that fate intervenes and saves your potentially awesome love story. Whatever type of books you like, the one common theme amongst all book lovers is we want to enjoy them. So, I hope you enjoy!

Table of Contents

Chapter One - The Stranger

It was a busy day at *The Beanery*. The thick, rich aroma of dark roast coffee delighted the customers as they waited to place their orders. The small, quaint coffee shop was located on one of the busiest streets in Kamiah. People from all over the small town dropped in frequently for their favorite cup of coffee or tea. One patron in particular, was a favorite among the young women who worked there. The baristas always smiled and gave each other looks whenever he entered the café'. It was an eerily calm and sunny day, and the shop was busier than ever. It was no surprise when the door chimed and in walked the mysterious stranger. They were expecting him. It seemed his visits were perfectly timed. He always showed up whenever Kamiah resident Giselle Jackson was there.

His appeal was instant. Magnetic. No one knew who the gentleman was and had only recently started seeing him around town. "Hi. May I help you," the young woman said. He looked her directly and deeply in her eyes. The woman smiled as she waited on the handsome and mysterious man. He ordered a small black coffee *to go* and then looked over towards Giselle's table. He looked back at the barista and gave her a devilish grin as she waited for his coffee. She flirted with him and then glanced over at her co-worker. The man didn't come in often. But he had been there enough times to cause quite a stir amongst the young female employees that worked there. His smooth, silky dark skin with sexy brown eyes and chiseled features were enough to melt anyone woman's heart.

The women had talked him up. He hadn't been there in over a week. The barista named Andrea had just asked about him. She was smitten and had been enquiring about him whenever she arrived to work. She told her fellow co-worker and friend Sara, that when he looked at her, she felt as though he was looking through her. Straight to her soul. She was taken with him and was hoping to catch his attention.

She had been daydreaming about him and longed to see him. What started out as an innocent crush had turned into something much more. Andrea desired him. She was trying to find the confidence to say something to him. She wanted to know more about him. But he was intimidating. He appeared preoccupied. Something had his undivided attention. His smiles and seemingly cool reserve could not cover the fact that he himself appeared to be smitten. And not with Andrea.

It hadn't gone unnoticed, that he started arriving whenever Giselle was there. That he watched her and hung around until she left. Andrea decided not to make her interest known. She wondered if the two had not started a love affair. With Grant frequenting the coffee shop as well, it made sense if they had decided to keep it a secret. It would explain Giselle's indifference, whenever the stranger was there. What the women didn't know was that although he appeared interested in Giselle, she was not interested in him. She did not know him. Not yet!

No one knew of him in their small town. People wondered if he was from Craigmont. A large city not too far away. Kamiah had a small population but had grown larger and more diverse over the years. The town had experienced an increase in population due to the presence of several large companies. Companies that decided to open satellite offices in an around the downtown area. People flocked to the picturesque town with its clean air and dense but beautiful forests. Local residents had noticed the stranger, but no one seemed to recall where from. He seemed to appear out of nowhere and had started being sought after for his carpentry skills. Word of mouth spread quickly with regards to his work and expert craftmanship. And gossip spread amongst the single women of Kamiah who sought to know him on a more intimate level. No one knew much about the man other than he was a handsome loner who did meticulous work and his name was Alonzo.

Giselle sat at a table with her laptop open, sipping on a Vanilla Bean Crème. She looked around at the other patrons and spoke to a few of the regulars that frequented the coffee shop. The place had been in business for twenty years and Giselle was a regular. She knew the owners. A large family that consisted of a husband, a wife and their five daughters. The atmosphere was perfect.

Giselle continued to sip her latte as she put the finishing touches on a spreadsheet for a board meeting the next morning. She glanced over and observed the handsome stranger. She had noticed the charismatic gentleman who seemed to be paying extra attention to her. His face wasn't familiar. Giselle figured he was new in town. She looked up several times, catching the man staring at her. He gazed intensely into her eyes, which made her uncomfortable and she looked away. Giselle couldn't help but notice the young woman flirting with him and chuckled to herself. She thought he was too mature for women in their early twenties and laughed at how hard they tried to get his attention. The man looked to be in his early thirties and had a tantalizing, magnetic appeal. He looked like something only a woman of a certain maturity could handle. There was nothing reserved or modest looking about him. He looked like a man that burned hot like a roaring flame.

But Giselle was much too busy to concern herself. She sipped from her Vanilla Bean Latte as she finalized her work. "There. I think that about covers it," she said, as she closed her laptop and tried to relax. She was done with her spreadsheet and it was the perfect time to take in the atmosphere. Something that she rarely did due to her hectic schedule. She put in long hours at *DataWorks Corporation.* An Information Technologies company where she worked her way up to become their senior programmer and web developer. Hard work and dedication had paid off for her. Giselle was a woman on the go and had worked hard enough to be featured in a local magazine called *Women on Top.*

She had everything going for her. Everything a woman could ask for, except a family. She had given up on marriage and children to focus on her career, which was thriving. The only child of Edward and Julie Jackson, Giselle had returned to Kamiah to live in her childhood home. She had extended family spread out in various states but no other relatives that lived in Kamiah. The closest family members lived over 25 miles away in the city of Craigmont.

"Anyone sitting here," Grant said, as he smiled at his ex-girlfriend. Giselle smiled and shook her head no then moved her things out of his way. Giselle was the love of his life. The one who got away, but not quite. They were childhood friends and went to high school together. They had noticed each other in school, but their budding romance was cut short when Giselle and her family moved away. They reconnected and started dating once Giselle returned to her birthplace. But Giselle's drive and strong independence drove a wedge between them. Grant was aggressive and wanted to control her and she pulled away to keep the peace. The relationship eventually stalled and the two were now occasional lovers. But Grant held out hope. He wanted to marry her. He wanted to have children with her. And so, he took all she had to offer with the hopes of one day winning her over.

"Hey. What you doing here?" she asked, scooting over to make room. "I knew you would be here," Grant replied, as he sat down and pulled a laptop from his briefcase. "I'll be back. I want a black decaf. You want anything else?" he asked. "No. I'm wired. I had a Vanilla Bean with a shot of

Espresso in it," she stated. Grant got up and walked to the counter as Giselle looked on. She smiled at him. She watched his walk. The way he handled himself. The way he innocently flirted with the young lady as he placed his order. Giselle was attracted to him and he was a great lover. She just wished he wasn't so demanding. She had to be in control of her life. He was looking for a stay at home woman who would be happy catering to him while he paid the bills. The type of woman she wasn't.

Giselle knew she would never be able to satisfy him and so she pulled back. She wasn't ready for the level of commitment he demanded. Grant had surrendered to a life of sex and nights on the town. He held out hope that one day she would open her heart to him. One day love him the way he loved her. But Giselle did have love for him. He had a special place in her heart. And she enjoyed him as a lover. He went all out and she liked the way he made her feel. If there was a man, whose last name she wouldn't mind taking, it would have been Grant Ellis'.

He was a handsome and brilliant man. The towns charismatic Sheriff and devoted Kamiah resident. He'd run for mayor in their last election but didn't win. He lost by a small margin and promised everyone he would run again. Grant was a woman's dream. Just not Giselle's. There were several women hoping to get a date with the town's sheriff and most eligible bachelor. But Grant had competition. A newcomer had everyone's attention. The town was buzzing with gossip about their newest resident. He was admired and sought after. The women of Kamiah had their eyes on him but he had eyes for only one woman. Giselle Jackson.

Giselle sipped her coffee as she read an article on web page development. She rubbed the back of her neck as she inhaled deeply. She looked up then back at her computer. She nervously fidgeted with a pen, then sat it down and rubbed her neck again. The shop felt suddenly warm. She shook her foot then crossed her legs as she tried to get more comfortable. *Why is it so hot,* she thought, as she exhaled sharply and continued reading the article. Soon she could no longer ignore that she was uncomfortable and her body was being overwhelmed with intense feelings. A familiar heat. One she hadn't felt in a long time. It was sexual in nature and she found herself in an awkward moment. She wanted to have sex at a time she wasn't thinking about sex. And the feeling was intense.

I need to relax, she thought, as she adjusted the way she sat. She wondered if it was that time. She could get horny when she started her monthly cycle. The pressure from the stiff cushioned chair could be aiding in what now seemed like an intense sexual desire.

Giselle began to feel hot. She sat her Vanilla Bean Latte down and looked around. Feelings of anxiety and embarrassment came over her. Her body felt weightless. She recognized the sensation, and the feeling was intensifying. *Damn! What is this? Why do I feel horny? Now! This is insane,* she thought, as she looked around. The feeling continued to intensify as it took hold. Giselle closed her eyes, wishing it would go away. This was the second time her body was reacting this way. The first time it happened was a few days prior as she lay in her bed. Giselle was mortified that she had no control over her body. All she could do was brace herself until the feeling went away.

A feeling of heat resonated throughout her body. A series of vibrations moved through her and she was powerless to its hold on her. Giselle had a healthy sexual appetite and would have enjoyed such feelings if she had been in the comforts of her home. But she was in a coffee shop. She wondered if anyone was watching. She looked around once more. The patron's that were there were preoccupied and not looking her way. Grant appeared to be in a serious conversation and was also not looking. Giselle's private area felt as if it had been manually stimulated. She placed her hands between her legs, since no one was close enough to see. Sitting on the opposite side of a small divider wall gave her enough privacy to touch herself quickly. *Are you fucking kidding me? What is going on with me,* she thought, as she sat there having one of the most powerful orgasms she'd ever had.

Giselle dropped her head and tried to calm herself as the feeling slowly faded away. She raised her head and looked around again. Grant glanced over at her and continued with his conversation. *What was that?* she thought, as she looked over at Grant talking and laughing with a gentleman. Giselle hastily gathered her things and walked toward Grant. "Hey. I got to go," she said, as she turned and walked away. Grant ended his conversation with his neighbor and followed Giselle out to the parking lot.

"Gi! Wait up," he said, as he walked behind her. Grant picked up the pace as Giselle appeared to be in a hurry. She walked quickly towards her car, never looking up at Grant or responding to his attempts at getting her attention. "What's wrong? I just got here. What's your hurry?" he asked. "Nothing Grant. I just... I got to go," she replied.

The tension was thick. Something strange and embarrassing had just happened. Giselle counted the minutes until she would be home. She got in her car and looked at Grant through the window. He stood there for a minute and Giselle finally rolled down her window to talk to him. "I felt sick all of a sudden Grant. It's nothing for you to be concerned about. I have to go. I'll call you tonight," she said, appearing jumpy and not at all her usual calm self. "Can I stop by later?" he asked. "Not tonight Grant. After I leave work, I'm going home and lie down. I'm exhausted," she replied. Grant hesitated then turned and walked back towards *The Beanery* as

Giselle watched. Her behavior had him confused. He could tell something had occurred and she wasn't talking. Grant knew not to push her buttons. If she didn't want to talk then she wouldn't until she was ready.

The car idled, as Giselle sat there unable to pull off. She was still in a daze about the powerful orgasm she had out of nowhere and for no real reason. She had just had sex with Grant a few days prior and was shocked at how powerful the feeling was. Giselle looked around. She gathered her composure then reached for her cell phone. "Ok. It's in here somewhere," she said, as she searched. Feelings of anxiety returned, as she searched the car for the phone. "Ok Giselle. Slow down. That phone has to be here somewhere. It didn't grow feet and jump out of the car. I had it. I know I did" she said, as she put her hands over her face. *Please! I just want to get out of here,* she said, as she kept her hands over her face. The thought of such an orgasm in public had embarrassed her. And the thought of having to go back inside *The Beanery*, looking for a phone, frustrated her.

Giselle took her hands away from her face. She immediately noticed that the handsome and mysterious man from inside the coffee shop was watching her. He paused then immediately got inside of a brand new black suburban and look at her again. It was the same man she saw standing at the counter. The man that the young women openly flirted with. The man who had already caught her attention, if but briefly. Giselle locked eyes with him, then looked away. Something about his stare was intense and familiar. Something about it seemed intimate. Giselle shrugged off his attentions and searched between the car seats, still trying to locate her cell phone. She glanced up at him briefly and continued searching. "Yes. Finally," she said, as she pulled it from the side of the drivers' seat and checked for missed calls and texts.

Giselle sat her phone down then glanced over at the suburban once more. The gentleman hadn't pulled off yet and appeared to be reading something. Giselle watched him. There was something about his aura. She felt drawn to him. She was attracted to him. There was something about him that had her curious. Something captivating that she couldn't put her hands on. The stranger looked up at Giselle and smiled before backing out of his parking space and pulling off. Giselle watched his car pull out of the parking lot and onto the street. She continued watching as though she was hypnotized. She watched until she could no longer see his car. *Who is he?* she thought, before grabbing her sunglasses and driving away.

"Hey," Grant said, as Giselle opened the door the next morning. She lived in a large contemporary home that her father and his company custom built. The house was beautiful and was nestled near the forest and mountains near a beautiful picturesque and serene lake. The cherrywood and stone trim home was magnificent, with its large beautiful windows and pristine landscaping. The house was most beautiful at night, as the indoor and outdoor lighting features gave the home a classy and sophisticated look. Giselle had lived in the home since she was a young girl and now it was hers. Her mother died when she was nineteen and her father died several years after.

"Hey," she replied, as she opened the door so he could walk in. "I was just coming to check on you. What happened Giselle? You looked like you'd seen a ghost and you didn't answer my calls last night," he said. "It was nothing Grant. I just felt ill suddenly. It was nothing," she replied. "You pregnant," he asked, hoping she was. "What? No. Maybe it was that Latte. I don't usually ask for an extra shot. Maybe that's what made me sick," she replied. "Don't you have to work today?" she asked, trying to change the subject, "No. I called off. I need a day to myself. We've been getting swamped with strange animal attacks and livestock killings and so we've been putting in extra hours trying to locate the bear or wolves responsible. With you up here in the mountains, it makes me worry Giselle. There are wolves and bears here. You are right in the middle of their home. You still have that shot gun I gave you?" he asked.

"Yes Grant. But I've lived here all my life and yes, I've seen a few bears and even a few wolves, but nothing has happened. Animals are safer than humans. You got what, two animal attacks this month. How many assault cases run across your desk?" she said sarcastically. Giselle loved animals and she didn't agree with Grant that they were dangerous and posed a big threat. She was used to elk, bears, deer's, rabbits and wolves around her home. She feared the bears the most, and used her shotgun to make a loud bang and scare them off if she felt threatened.

"I missed you though. I took off so I could see you. Want to go boating? We could go fishing," he suggested, hoping she would spend time with him. Giselle walked away from him and pondered his suggestion. It was a Saturday and she had no immediate plans. "Ok. But no fishing. Let's just go on the water," she replied. Giselle walked toward her master bedroom and into her bath. She jumped in the shower as Grant sat on her couch turning channels. He sat there and thought about going to her room and trying to make love to her but he didn't want to risk her rejecting him and changing her mind. He wanted her and he hoped after a full day of being together, she would indulge him and allow him to give her pleasures that he thought, only he could give her.

After a long day out on the boat, Grant and Giselle decided to eat in, relax and watch a movie. Giselle plopped down on her couch and then Glanced over looking for Grant. He had excused himself and left to use the restroom. "Oh. That looks like it may be good," she said, as she watched the trailer to a movie she decided to watch. Grant walked into her kitchen and grabbed his plate then joined Giselle on the couch. The smell of apples and cinnamon resonated throughout her meticulous and well-designed home. Giselle loved plug in scented oils and had them scattered throughout. Grant looked at Giselle then smiled as he took a bite of his pita wrapped chicken sandwich. He put his arm around her shoulder and pull her closer to him.

Giselle always like spending time with Grant. He could be charming when he wanted and she liked having him around. There had been times in the past when she had considered how much easier and safer her life would be if she had a man around. But she wasn't ready to get started on another serious commitment with him. They had been down that road several times in the past, with the same ending. For now, she was content to let things be and allow them to just enjoy what they have. A close bond.

It was a daunting task for Giselle to get on her Craftsman riding mower and cut the lawn. She'd learned how to repair things herself over the years so that she wouldn't have to depend on anyone else. She wanted to do traditional women tasks like cook, clean, please her man and take on the world. Not fix leaky sinks and cut tall grass. But Giselle was a strong, beautiful and independent woman. She looked more like a model and not at all like the type to do manual labor around the house. But her father raised her to be independent and self-sufficient and so she hated to play the victim and lean on the skills of a man. So, she sighed and climbed on top of her craftsman and mowed the lawn. It took her nearly an hour to get the main areas cut. Grant had volunteered to cut and manicure the lawn but Giselle wouldn't allow it. The two of them worked on the landscaping for several hours before retiring into her home.

It was getting dark and after taking a quick shower, Giselle sat next to Grant. She eventually fell asleep laying on his shoulder as he continued to watch tv. He kissed her on her head and she woke up and looked at him. They stared at each other and Grant got closer to her face and kissed her softly on the lips. Giselle didn't say a word and he kissed her again. The two embraced in a passionate and fervent kiss, as they touched each other's bodies and pulled on each other clothes. Grant looked out her window. Something caught his attention. He thought he saw something in the brush but didn't want to alarm Giselle. "Let's go to the room," he said. "What? Why?" she replied. Grant looked again but didn't see anything and the two of them embraced again, in a deep and passionate kiss.

Grant was always uncomfortable with the openness of Giselle's tall uncovered windows that gave outsiders a clear view. Especially at night, when it was more difficult to see the surrounding area. But Giselle was used to it. And she often walked around naked in her house since she had no neighbors close by. "No. Let's do it right here," she said, not wanting to kill the mood and wanting him at that very second. Grant glanced out the window again, still concerned with what he was sure was movement in the bushes. Grant became less concerned with the outside as Giselle's frisky behavior was impossible to ignore.

After glancing outside once more, he dove his tongue inside her mouth. He kissed her with fierce passion and moaning as she grabbed his manhood through his pants. "I want you Grant. I've been horny lately. I needed you the other day," she said, as she continued kissing him. Grant reached down to unzip his pants but stopped abruptly when he heard a loud thud. A noise that sounded like a metal can crashing to the ground. "What the fuck was that," he said, as he jumped up and ran to the window. "Cut the lights off. I see something near the trees," he said. Giselle cut off the lights then went and stood next to him. They could see something huge in the shrubs near the trees. "What is that. Is that a wolf?" he said, as he thought he saw the silhouette of what looked like a huge dog.

Grant thought his eyes were deceiving him. Wolves were not that big. The animal looked massive and he struggled to make sense of what he was seeing. "What Grant. I don't see anything," Giselle said, as her eyes scanned the edge of the forest. "Go get your shotgun," Grant said. "No. You're not shooting at something and you don't even know what it is," she replied. "It's a huge wolf. You don't see it. It's right there," he said, pointing in the direction. "No. I don't see anything," she said, as she continued looking around. "That's probably the one that's been killing animals around here. Where's the shotgun?" he said.

"I'm not getting it. You are not killing an innocent animal at my house Grant. I live here, not you. Shoot animals on your own property," she said. Grant walked away as Giselle stood there looking out into the wilderness. She looked around and thought she saw what looked like a bear. Grant walked back in and opened her glass sliding door. "What are you doing. Give me that," she yelled. Grant took aim and fired before Giselle could get the gun from him and watched as the animal ran. "There! You see him now. He's running," he blurted.

"What is your problem," she said, as she shook her head and turned to go in the house.

Grant came in and closed the sliding door slowly. "Why are you mad. I didn't hit it. But now, its probably scared. I doubt it comes back," he said, as it was obvious, she was highly upset. "You should go. I'm tired," she said. "Giselle… You want me to go. I had to fire the gun. That thing was massive. I probably should have killed it. It was a wolf. Probably the one killing animals. People are losing livestock. Don't be mad" he pleaded. "Grant please!" she said, as she got up from the couch, walked in her bedroom and shut her door. Grant sighed as he walked back to her closet and placed her gun inside. He thought for a moment about going into her room and trying to get her to forgive him. But Giselle was the type of woman you had to let be.

He paused before opening the door and stepping out into the breeze of the cool night. He looked up and admired the bright full moon that lit up the ground and surrounding area. His mood was melancholy and somber. Giselle being upset with him was yet another wedge between them. He was losing ground with her. It seemed as though he could not win with her and wondered why that was. Grant took his time getting to his car and looked around, still aware that an animal had been close by. When he approached his car, he pulled out his keys then stopped and looked around.

He thought he heard something behind him, but brushed it off and unlocked his doors. Before he could grab the handle, he quickly turned around. Grant stood in shock as a huge, massive black wolf walked slowly his way. He stood, filled with fear, as the wolf with a white patch on its nose growled menacingly at him. He grabbed his key and hit the panic alarm hoping the sound would scare it off, but the animal was undeterred.

The wolf continued to advance. His head lowered. His teeth completely exposed. The animal was preparing to attack and Grant was paralyzed with fear. Giselle, hearing the commotion, opened her door and stepped out on the porch. "Giselle. Go get the gun now," he said. Giselle looked at the wolf and her eyes got big. She hesitated and it turned around and looked at her. She looked the animal in its eyes and the wolf ran off into the woods. Grant was breathing heavily and now mad at Giselle for hesitating again. "So, you were going to let that thing attack me?" he fumed. "No. I was just in shock. I've never seen one that big. Ever. I was going to get the gun," she said, as he got into his car. Grant looked at her and shook his head as he pulled off.

Chapter Two - Watched

The next morning Giselle got up early and fixed herself breakfast. She opened several windows, including her glass sliding door. The door was secured by a sliding screen that she kept closed. She looked out into the forest thinking of the wolf she had seen the night before. She was still surprised at its size. She was surprised to see that it had a distinct white patch of hair above its nose. She remembered seeing a wolf with that same patch as a young girl and then again, as a teenager.

When she was just ten years old, a black wolf with the same white patch approached her. She was sitting on a log and playing with her dolls when it approached her slowly from behind. Her father was outside cutting the lawn and trimming trees close to their house when he looked up and panicked when he couldn't see Giselle. She was playing and got a little deeper in the woods than she was allowed to go. Her father, after noticing she was no longer within view, jumped off his lawn mower and started calling her name. For a moment he assumed she went back inside the house. He heard her scream and went running with his shotgun.

By the time he reached Giselle, the wolf had gotten so close, that he feared taking the shot. He didn't want to risk hitting Giselle. He told her to slowly back away, but when she moved and the wolf moved with her. The father aimed his gun hoping that if Giselle would continue to back away, there would be a safe enough distance between them to fire. But the wolf stayed close to her. Giselle father steadied his aim as he continued instructing Giselle to walk backwards. He looked down the barrel and then dropped it slightly when to his astonishment, the wolf licked her face. Giselle touched his nose and he licked her hand. "No Gi. No," he urged, as he raised his gun again. The animal, with his intimidating size as he towered over Giselle, seemed gentle. But her father wanted the animal gone. He wanted to kill it. If it was comfortable enough to get close, then that made the animal unpredictable. It would return. Something he couldn't chance.

"No!" he shouted as Giselle tried to touch the wolf once more. The loud shout from her father spooked the wolf and caused him to run. He fired one shot, missing the wolf and Giselle screamed *no*. She was upset that her father would try to hurt the animal. What her father didn't know was Giselle had observed the wolf before. Initially, terrified due to his size, she stayed away from the deep part of the forest. But after an encounter, when the animal smelled her then ran, she became less fearful of him.

Giselle was a natural animal lover. There were many occasions when she caught rabbits and even frogs from the lake. She had a fascination with them which worried her father. She had a trusting nature that sometimes brought her into harm's way. She promised she would never bring harm to an animal. She told herself that animals were not the problem. She believed that if you let them be, they would stay away. That they were basically more afraid of humans. And she carried that belief with her into adulthood.

A second encounter happened years later with what looked like the same wolf. It occurred just weeks before her family moved away to Canada when Giselle was a teenager. Giselle was outdoors, on a beautiful fall day, helping her father gather wood. She leisurely picked up wood and placed it in a wagon, looking around and taking in the scenery. Giselle seemed to be daydreaming as she picked a daisy and pulled her wagon closer to the edge of the forest. The forest was a great source of large, fallen branches. Just the size her father hoped to gather. He had told her to look for large pieces only. He was yards away, picking up what he could as he occasionally glanced over at his daughter. Giselle looked over at her father then advanced deeper past the trees. She ended up out of view and she hadn't noticed how far she had gone in.

The wood was plentiful since a storm has ripped through the area a few days prior. Giselle picked up the pieces as she occasionally glanced up. She saw her father walking back to the house. She continued, determined to fill up her wagon. As she was bending over to gather more wood a crackle sound was heard in the distance. Giselle looked up but didn't see anything. She bent over to pick up a branch and stood up then dropped everything in her arms. She panicked at the sight of a black wolf with a white patch on its nose. He stood staring at her. She froze and looked around. Her father was now back at the house and she was defenseless. She looked at the closest tree and braced herself to run for it. The wolf walked slowly towards her and she looked around at the trees but none were close enough.

"Please go away," she said, as the wolf took a few steps closer. Giselle became emotional as she feared for her life. She started to cry as she begged the wolf to leave. She hoped he would run out of fear. She believed he was the same wolf that licked her when she was younger, although she wasn't sure. After several minutes, the wolf walked in front of her and sat down. His size now more ominous. It was large. It was as big as a bear and could have killed her in a fraction of a second. Giselle closed her eyes. Whatever was going to happen, she felt helpless. Her nerves took control of her. She prayed as she prepared for a possible attack. She looked back at her house, but her father was still nowhere in sight.

But there was something about his demeanor. Something tender. As if he was her long-lost dog. A familiarity that she sensed he felt with her. Confused and anxious, her body began to shake uncontrollably. And no matter how calm the moment seemed, his size could not be ignored. She was familiar with animals. Familiar with wolves. She had never witnessed one that size. And just as she turned her attention back to her house, he smelled her hand then licked it. Giselle looked at him. She reached out slowly to touch his nose and he licked her hand again. She took her other hand and rubbed the wolf and smiled. Her fears were vanished as it was apparent that the wolf would not be attacking.

Giselle continued petting him and then sat on a log and the animal laid in front of her while she rubbed his stomach. "Where are you from? Are you someone's pet?" she said, as she rubbed the animal. She looked back at her house and saw her father coming out. "Go. Don't let him see you," she said.

"The animal got up and ran into the woods as Giselle watched. She smiled then walked back to her home.

Giselle always looked for the wolf after that. Taking food to the forest and sitting it near her favorite tree. She would go back and check to see if the food was gone and it never was. She tried to hang around and hide behind trees, hoping to catch it eating but never could. But as Giselle reflected on the wolf from her past, she realized there was a distinct difference with the one she saw the night before. The one that approached Grant was much larger and seemed more menacing than the gentle one from her childhood. She remembered that wolf as larger than normal but the one that was ready to attack was even larger. But deep down, she believed it was possible. That it was the same wolf.

Giselle walked into the kitchen and made a pot of tea to drink with her toast and eggs. She sat at her table and opened her lap top. She looked at emails and checked her itinerary for upcoming events and important meetings. It was a peaceful and relaxing atmosphere as she sat in her robe. She sipped tea and enjoyed the serene ambiance of the wilderness as she glanced out the window. *I can't put it off any longer*, she thought, as she glanced over at her outdoor garden that had started to look sparse. Giselle sighed and finished up her tea and went to take a shower. She decided this was the day she would get her garden together.

"Hey Giselle," Mrs. Timmons said, as she greeted her neighbor who lived five miles up the road. "Hello Mrs. Timmons," she replied, smiling and looking around. Giselle was a regular. She loved flowers and she frequented Mrs. Timmons nursery regularly. "You need help. I have to ask even though I already know you know these flowers better than I do," she said, walking with Giselle toward the perennials. "No. I'm going to start here and grab a few things then go over to the annuals," she replied.

The huge beautiful nursery was Giselle's favorite spot. She walked around past a large, dense area of shrubs and trees and slowly made her way towards the back of the nursery. She started feeling hot and tense and reached down to unzip her fanny pack so she could put her sunglasses on. *Oh my. It's hot out here. Not one cloud in the sky,* she thought, as she continued walking. It was middle of summer and the day was extra hot with temperatures close to ninety degrees. "Giselle. Here you go. I know it's hot out here. I saw you put on your sunglasses. Sorry we don't have much natural shade at this back part of the nursery," Mrs. Timmons said, as she handed Giselle a bottled water. "Thanks," she said, as she immediately opened it and took a sip.

Rugged cut off jean shorts and plaid short sleeve button down shirts was her usual *go to* attire when not at work. She had taken the shirt and tied it in a knot. Giselle liked to dress with flair and would take old clothes and style them to add a chic appeal. "Hey Giselle," Mr. Timmons said, as he passed her. "Hey Mr. Timmons. How are you?" she replied. Giselle stopped right in front of the potted perennials and started looking at them one by one. She wiped her forehead and continued glancing over the large selection, as Mr. Timmons brought her a wagon to place them in. "Here you go," he said, as he parked it a few feet from her and walked away. Giselle looked at the wagon then quickly looked up at the shrubs when she noticed something moving. She stared for a moment, but brushed it off as possibly a racoon or squirrel. The perennials were in long rows and Giselle decided to thoroughly look through them. She was hoping to find one's that wouldn't spread like weeds or turn into a nightmare to control down the line. She had planted annuals the year before. She didn't want a perennial flower that would invade everything around it.

Giselle walked down the first aisle but continued to glance over at the shrubs and trees. She felt something was watching and following her. "Giselle. You sure you don't want me to help you select some things," Mrs. Timmons yelled. "No. I'm fine," she replied. Giselle continued to get spooked. She felt the presence of something lurking and started to get nervous. Giselle grabbed pots of Coneflowers, Coral Bells and Thistles and placed them in her wagon.

She continued shopping, occasionally glancing into the dense shrubs to see if she could catch a glimpse of whatever was hiding. "Oh these are nice," she said as she grabbed a few pots of Peonies. After a few more minutes, she decided to headed back to the checkout area. The strange and tense feeling was hard to ignore. "Are you alright Giselle. You look like you've seen a ghost," Mrs. Timmons commented. "It's the sun. I just need to get home and cool down before I start planting," she said. "I'll help you load those," Mr. Timmons said, as he retrieved the wagon and made his way to her olive green Jeep 4X4.

Giselle continued looking back at the shrubs as Mrs. Timmons rang up the flowers. Giselle handed Mr. Timmons her car keys so he could begin loading the flowers in her car. "Ok Giselle. That'll be one hundred eighty six dollars and ninety eight cents," she said, noticing that Giselle wasn't paying her any attention and was fixated on the shrubs behind her. "You need a shrub too. You have acres of shrubs and trees on your property. You probably don't need to plant any from what I remember," she advised. "Oh no. I was just looking," she said, reaching into her fanny pack and pulling her money out. "Here you go. Keep the change," she said. "Thanks Giselle. Gary has everything loaded for you. I'll see you soon," Mrs. Timmons said, as the women smiled at one another.

Giselle's intuition was right. Her feelings were dead on. Something was watching her from the shrubs. It had been watching her since she was ten years old and had started watching her more frequently. He longed for her and was determined to make his move. She had been marked and he was coming to claim her as his.

The radio played a nice soft melody as Giselle hummed to the tune. Music was a nice stress release from her hectic life. She rode the rough and rugged road back to her home still feeling tense and slightly off. She drove through the tall dense trees on her private road toward her home. A road that was filled with rock and debris. She slowed down as she normally did on the graveled drive. It was leveled but not perfectly and could damage her tires if she wasn't careful. Out of nowhere and without warning, her tire blew and she fought to gain control of the car. Giselle got control and then pulled over to the side. She rolled the car slowly before coming to a stop in dense vegetation. "Shit," she blurted, as she sighed then looked around. She paused then got out of her car and looked around. She walked to the back of her car to check the rear tire. She saw that tire was intact and then walked around to the passenger side and saw her rear tire was blown.

"Damn. Great," she said, in a low voice before opening the back door of her Jeep. Giselle look around for the car jack. She pulled the spare out then saw the jack underneath a piece of cardboard. "Oh good," she said, elated that she had what she needed. But changing a tire was something Grant or a tow company always did for her. She had been through a few tires due to her rough road. And she was not looking forward to the daunting task. Giselle walked to the rear tire and bent down to position the jack. She heard what sounded like, the snap of a stick in the tall grass behind her. Her nerves set in. It was dark and that made her vulnerable. She stopped and stood up and began to fear someone was there. She was still spooked from her visit at the nursery and was now on *full-on* alert.

After looking around and not seeing anything, she bent over and began pushing on the jack. The car raised up slowly. She grew tired quickly in the heat and opened her car door to grab her phone so she could call Grant. She didn't see her phone right away and wondered if it was in the back with the flowers. Giselle shut the door and turned around. She took a deep breath and swallowed. She stood paralyzed with fear. Standing before her was a large gray and white, six foot wolf staring at her. The animal was in a crouched position, growling as if ready to attack. It walked slowly towards her. Giselle began to tear up and was overcome with fear. Her hands shook as she raised them up hoping the animal wouldn't attack. "Ok. Easy boy," she said, as she slowly walked toward the back of her Jeep where she had a small hand gun hidden in a compartment.

The wolf moved closer and she stopped. Giselle knew that movement would cause it to move faster, but to stand there was certain death. She was no match for a small wolf let alone the massive six foot, one hundred and eighty pound wolf standing in front of her. The sound of crushed leaved and snapped branched could be heard in the distance. The wolf turned around, but immediately turned back to Giselle. She watched as shrubs and vegetation moved swiftly. Something was running towards them. A brief clearing of the vegetation revealed a massive, nearly seven foot two hundred and thirty pound black wolf, charging towards them. Giselle began to cry. She believed they were attacking as a pack. She tried to run for the back door causing the gray wolf to charge her. Seconds before he jumped in the air to bring her down, the large black wolf attacked it from behind. A fierce battle ensued as the gray wolf tried to keep up but was no match. He tried to run away from the much larger alpha male but the black wolf was merciless as he pounced on the grey wolf.

Giselle jumped in her car as they fought in the vegetation, unable to see the battle that was ensuing. The gray wolf tried to get away again. But every time it ran a few feet further, the black wolf attacked it again. A behavior that was unusual for wolves. Attacks of this nature usually ended fairly quickly if the beta wolf submitted. But the attack continued. Giselle calmed herself then realized she still had a major issue. She could not drive away.

She heard the whimpered cries of the gray wolf. The black wolf finally ceased attacking and allowed the gray wolf to leave. The black wolf emerged from the vegetation and stood a few feet from the Jeep looking at Giselle. Giselle was filled with fear even though she sat, protected inside her car. *Where's my phone,* she thought, as she got up and crawled to the back seat. She looked all around and was excited at finding it, only to realized she couldn't use it.

Dammit! she said, angry at herself for her phone having practically no battery life left. She only had a short time of battery life and had no way to charge it. Giselle looked at the call log and saw she had missed several calls from Grant and called him back. She looked at the phone. *Oh fuck. This is the bad area. I can't get a signal right here,* she said.

She looked up the road. She sighed at the thought that just a short distance up the road, there would be a signal. Giselle began to cry again and looked out the window. She stared at the wolf who was now laying on the ground like he didn't have a care in the world. "Go away," she said, as she looked around. She looked at her phone as if it would ring and her problems would be over. When she looked back towards the trees, the wolf was gone. She turned her head quickly, searching for him. "Where did he go that fast?" she said, continuing to look through the grass and surrounding area. It was turning dusk and it would be night soon. Her house was a two minute drive up the road and approximately five minutes by foot.

Giselle was terrified to get out and change the tire. She felt she had a better chance of trying to get home. She knew she would probably have a hard time getting the tires off. She figured it would take her even longer to change a tire versus jog to her house. She sat there as dusk turned to night and she looked around. She worried with each passing minute as darkness was inevitable. Her phone was now completely dead and she had to make a decision.

"The gun!" she said, as she crawled to the back and grabbed her small 22 caliber gun. She looked at it. Giselle sat there and sighed then quickly raised up. She knew that a 22-caliber handgun would not bring down a wolf. Especially the large ones that she saw. "I have no choice. Ok. Where's my flashlight," she said, looking out to the sky. It was now dark. There was zero visibility in certain areas, especially near the towering trees that lined her path. But there a full moon. It was bright enough to light the area closer to her home. But walking the road to get there would be terrifying. Giselle grabbed her flashlight. She had to try. She had no choice.

Giselle opened the door slowly and got out the car and quietly closed the door. She felt something was still out there and it was probably near. Wolves didn't stray far from prey and if something wanted her, it was simply waiting. She stood at her car door for several minutes trying to see if emerging from the car would draw it out. When she didn't see or hear anything, she took a deep breath. She proceeded up the rocky, but cleared path to her home. Looking around as she took slow, methodical steps. She sped up, walking faster then began jogging. It wasn't long before she was running as fast as she could. She slowed when she got tired then jogged for a few minutes before stopping to catch her breath.

When she stopped, she heard the crackling noise of branches and turned her flash light on. She pointed it in all directions terrified that one of the wolves had returned. "Please…Please," she whispered. She searched around moving quickly with the flashlight before stopping at an area of brush that was moving. She pointed the gun and kept her light on the bush. She was petrified at the sight of the large black wolf walking slowly out the bush toward her.

A tear rolled down from fear and she closed her eyes briefly. She stared at the wolf then tried to aim the gun at its eyes. She hoped she could shoot and injure it enough to make it home before the animal could catch her. Her father had taught her how to shoot guns, but this was at night and the target was moving. The wolf came closer and Giselle started to sweat from anxiety. The wolf got close enough to attack then sat down and stared at her. Giselle stared at it for a moment, squinting her eyes, perplexed at its demeanor and lack of aggression. It was huge. Capable of taking her down, even with a well-placed shot unless she got lucky.

Giselle lowered her gun and the Wolf got up and approached her and sat right in front of her. He sat there for several minutes then sniffed her hand. Giselle was still gripped in fear and thought he was just sizing her up and smelling his next meal. But there was something calm about the animal. She put the gun in her waist and reached her hand out and the wolf smelled then licked her hand.

The large animal stood up and got closer and smelled her crotch. "Stop," she said, as she pushed his nose away. The wolf then turned and trotted toward her house. He stopped and looked back at her. Giselle was confused and still full of fear. She stood there afraid to move. She noticed that the wolf stood there as if he was waiting on her. She hesitated and looked around then slowly walked on the path and the wolf turned and continued.

She sped up and looked around as she realized he was walking a direct path to her house. And she also realized that she was now following him. She began to feel safe. He was not attacking her. She was convinced he was domesticated. Somehow trained and brought up around people. *This must be someone's pet. Someone made a house pet out of a wolf?* she thought, as she continued up the road. The wolf walked off the path and through the vegetation as he neared her home. Giselle sped up and walked towards her home and looked back for him when she approached.

Giselle could see that the animal was following her. The wolf dropped back but was still within a few feet from her. She worried about the other aggressive gray wolf that was seconds from attacking her. But felt safe with the black wolf. She calmed down. "Am I being escorted home by an oversized, domesticated wild animal. Unbelievable," she thought, as she continued her brisk walk getting closer and closer to her house.

The wolf occasionally slowed, then would continue his much faster pace. Allowing her to stay in front of him versus falling behind. She reached her house and the wolf ran towards the woods and disappeared into the trees. Giselle walked up to her door and entered then looked out the window to see if it would reappear. *What just happened! I did not just get escorted home by a wolf!*

"Giselle, Mr. Garner wants to see you," the secretary said, as she peeked her head into her office. Giselle was sitting in her office, still in a fog about the events of the night before. She had been on her computer all morning researching wolves, their habits, habitats and behavioral patterns. "Yep. Can you tell him I'll be there in a minute," she said, as she read an article about wolf activity in her area.

"Yes," Giselle said to Mr. Garner, as she walked in his office. "The report you turned in this morning seemed to be missing information Giselle. I'm used to a much more thorough and detailed report on our clients. I need it to contain information on the systems they have and how we can sell them on an upgrade," he said, looking sternly at her. "I know. I'm sorry Mr. Garner. I had a busy and frightening weekend that spooked me and I just couldn't concentrate. Last night I caught a flat and had to wait until this morning to get my car towed. I can redo the reports. I can have them ready by morning. Give me one more day," she said, looking at him, but then glancing out the window as a feeling of sexual intensity came over her. Something had her feeling warm and excited inside and it was so sudden, that she questioned if something was in the coffee she'd just drank.

"Well I expect the revised report first thing. I know you can do better," Mr. Garner stated. Giselle walked over to his window and looked down. They were on the fifth floor and she could faintly see a man in the distance. He appeared to be looking at her, which would have been impossible. She could barely make him out from the vantage point and lighting, so she was sure he was in an even worse position. She could see he was a dark-skinned, tall man but not much else. She could faintly hear Mr. Garner talking as she had already tuned him out. She was distracted. The man continued to look up at her and she was curious. *Who is that?* she thought, as she watched him.

"Huh. You say something," she said, as she turned to Mr. Garner. "Yes, I did. I was trying to tell you about our meeting with *Fluid Inc*. They just want to see specs of why they should change IT companies. Then we're pretty much going to be given that account," he said. "Oh yeah," Giselle said, turning her attention back to the gentleman down below. "Ok. Let me get going. I'll probably get this done faster and with less stress if I work from home. If there's nothing else, I'll be leaving shortly," she said. Mr. Garner told her to take off whenever she was ready but to have the revised report to him by nine o'clock that next morning.

Giselle waited at the light to cross the street. It was lunch time and the streets were full. Coupled with the fact that one of the city's major freeways was closed for construction, had the streets busier than usual. *Ok. I'll relax a moment, sip on a latte then head home,* she thought, as she walked toward *The Beanery Coffee Shop*. She hadn't been to her favorite place to relax in several weeks. She planned on getting her usual latte, relaxing then getting home to complete the proposal. "Hi.

Welcome back. What can I get you?" the familiar face said, as Giselle looked up at their menu.

"Um. Let me get a Vanilla Latte and one of your blueberry muffins," she replied. She searched her purse, looking for her money which she sometimes tossed loosely inside. Giselle pulled the crumbled dollars out and tried to straighten them as she felt a breath on her neck. She turned her head and locked eyes with the same man she could have sworn was watching from the street below her bosses' window. She realized that it was also the same handsome, sexy and mysterious man that had been frequenting *The Beanery* recently. The man that the women baristas had a crush on. "Sorry. I'm uh, I'm almost done," she said nervously, as he stared at her with a smile. "Take your time," he said.

Giselle turned back around and the barista smiled and gave her a; *Yes. We know. He makes us nervous too,* look. She waited for Giselle to pay her and glanced at the gentleman. She smiled at him and then turned her attention back to Giselle. Giselle fumbled nervously before handing the barista all the singles she had in her hand and walking away. She sat at her favorite table and the woman came over and handed her the change. "You paid too much. Here's your change," she said. "I'm sorry. Thanks."

The woman started to walk away and Giselle called to her. "Wait! Excuse me. Do you know who that man is?" she asked. "No. I wish. I've never seen such a handsome and intriguing man in my life. We talk about him and count the days until he enters," she said, giggling like a school girl. "He just recently started coming here. But he comes here a lot. The funny thing is so do you. At first, we thought he was a friend or new coworker of yours. But you never spoke to him or even acknowledged his presence, so we figured that wasn't so," she continued.

"Why would you think I knew him?" Giselle asked. "Well. Because he only comes in here when you're in here. We've never seen him and you weren't already here. You never noticed him?" the barista asked. "I mean. No. Not until, like recently. But I'm always busy. I have a lot going on. But..." Giselle acknowledged. "Are you saying you think he's following me?" she asked. "Oh no. We didn't think that. It just seems like he comes when you're here. Maybe he likes you and can see when you come here. Maybe he works at one of the offices across the street. I don't know. I just find it coincidental," she replied.

"What's your name again? I know you've told me before, but I'm terrible with names," she said. "It's Andrea," the barista replied. Giselle watched as the man got his coffee and exited without looking over at her. Not even a glance. He sipped his coffee and walked toward his car. Andrea walked away and Giselle watched as the man got into a black Suburban and pulled off. *Wow. He's really handsome!*

Chapter Three - Beastly

Giselle walked into her house and kicked her shoes off. She relaxed and lounged as she waisted time. She found it hard to focus. It was hard to get the energy needed to complete her work. She stressed because she had only partially completed the spreadsheet she promised for the next morning. She could do them with her eyes closed, but something had her stressed. She never burned out or was too lazy to complete her projects.

She was at the top of her game. One of the best. It was the reason why she was paid nearly a hundred and twenty five thousand dollars a year plus bonuses. She went into her kitchen and grabbed an apple then walked over to her dining room. She sat at the table and pulled her laptop from her case. It was dusk outside and though she didn't worry about the spreadsheet and report, she wanted it off her plate so she could enjoy the rest of her evening. "Ok Giselle. Stop lollygagging and focus. Let's do this," she said, as she opened up the proposal and began to type. After several hours she shut her laptop and stretched her arms. It was complete and she could relax.

Just as she made her way up the modern looking, decorative and short staircase to her room, she heard a knock at the door. *Are you serious. That has to be Grant. Who else would just show up,* she thought. "Who is it?" she yelled, as she walked back down the stairs. "It's me. Grant," he said. Giselle rolled her eyes then opened the door. "Grant. What are you doing here? You should have called first. I'm tired and I have to get some rest. I have a big day tomorrow. We talked about this," she complained, as she stood there blocking his entry.

"Check your phone Giselle. I did call," he said, as he moved her arm and walked into her house. "Grant. Please. I don't feel like company," she said, looking seriously at him and walking back to her door. "I'm not staying long. I just wanted to talk to you. Give me a minute," he said, as he sat at her table. Giselle sat in the chair next to him. "What is it?" she asked. Grant wanted to make love to her. He wanted to stay the night and he wanted to ask her about what one of the women at *The Beanery* had told him.

"Is it true. That some guy has been following you around. There aren't any new residents that fit his description that I personally know about. No one knows this guy yet he's fixated on you. Comes in the coffee shop whenever you do. Stares at you. Usually leaves after you leave," he said, looking her directly in her eyes. "Grant. That man is free to go wherever he wants to. That's not true. I've only seen him a few times. I wouldn't say he's following me," she replied, shaking her head at the thought that the man was some type of problem.

Grant was jealous. He believed the man was the reason for Giselle recent lack of attention towards him. "Tell the truth Giselle. Are you seeing this guy or what?" he asked. "I don't owe you an explanation of what I do. You have no right to be jealous. And for your information, no. I'm not. I don't even know him," she replied, now angered by the jealousy he was showing. She didn't like him showing up to confront her about her personal life. She fought to get an understanding with him. That they were lovers, not husband and wife. That what she did in her spare time was her personal business. And that if she was seeing someone, he had no right to confront her about it.

Grant looked away and then back at her and stood up, ready to leave. There was something about her attitude he didn't recognize. Giselle was usually more flirtatious and would have wanted him sexually by this time. She wasn't this cold and distant. She appeared to be bothered by his visit, something she had never done before. And they hadn't made love in weeks which was unusual. Giselle was a sexual woman and required frequent intercourse. Grant walked towards her door then turned around and walked back to her. Giselle took a step back.

"Of course I'm jealous. I still love you. I came here to be with you. But I know you're tired so I'll let you rest. I want to see you tomorrow. I need you Gi," he said, as he reached out and touched her face "Ok. But call me," she hesitated. They had grown further apart and she couldn't explain it. She didn't desire him. She just wasn't ready to tell him.

Giselle stood in her door and watched as he walked toward his car. She saw him slow up and stare at the hood. "What the fuck," he shouted, as he stood there. "What?" she yelled. "There's a dead rabbit on the hood of my car," he shouted. Grant walked back on the porch and past Giselle. "So, you not seeing anyone Giselle. What the fuck! Who would do that. I've only been in here a few minutes. Who would do that?" he shouted. "I don't know. What do you mean? I'm not seeing anyone and if I was, I wouldn't date someone who would do something so heartless. You know how I feel about animals," she replied, looking out at his car puzzled by what had happened.

Grant stared at her. He fumed at the thought that someone had vandalized his car with an animal carcass. And a part of him didn't believe Giselle had no idea who it was. She was acting strange. She was different. And he believed he knew why. He had an idea. He believed it was the man that everyone had told him about. Her man. The new man in her life. The one that was the reason he could no longer make love to her. "Giselle I'm warning you. If we bump heads it won't be good," he said. "Grant. You don't own me. You wouldn't bump into anyone if you called me first before you just stopped by. I told you the truth and really, I don't owe you anything," she said, as she slipped her house shoes on. "Where are you going?" he asked. "To get the rabbit off your car and bury it. I don't want to smell it's rotting carcass. Plus, the smell will draw more animals."

Giselle walked around the back of her house and went into her shed. Grant stood near his car looking at the hood. It was covered in blood and she shook his head in disbelief. Giselle couldn't see the shovel in the dark and so she turned on the lights. She was startled at the sight of the massive black wolf standing in her shed. She stood there, paralyzed with fear but then calmed down. The animal just stood there looking at her. "Gi. You ok," Grant shouted, as he began to walk toward the shed. "Yeah. I'm ok. I was just looking for my shovel. Here I come," she said, as she grabbed the shovel and quickly exited and closed the door.

"What were you doing? It's dark out here. There are bears and wolves out here," he said. Giselle walked towards his car and knocked the rabbit off with the shovel. "Great. You scratched my car," he said. "You have a better way to remove it. I'm all ears," she said, as she picked it up with the shovel and carried it to the grass. Giselle found a soft spot and began to dig. "Give me that," Grant said, as he took the shovel and finished digging. He placed the rabbit in the hole and covered it with dirt. "There," he said, handing her the shovel.

"Listen Gi. I need you to be more careful. There have been sightings of a large pack of wolves. We have kill orders on them. They haven't attacked a person yet, but they're responsible for the death of livestock. The town is demanding something be done," he warned. "Really. So that's the solution. Not capture and send to a reserve, but shoot to kill. When they are only behaving naturally in their environment. Whatever! Tell your men don't come around here playing cowboy with the animals on my property. We will have a problem. I have a no trespassing sign. I expect them to honor it. The animals that live on my land have been given my permission to trespass. Your men do not have my permission," she cautioned. "Don't be like that Giselle. It's for your protection too," he replied. She looked at him with contempt and turned and walked back toward her house. "Can I still call you tomorrow," he shouted. "No."

Giselle sat on her couch, for over an hour, thinking of the wolf in her large shed. She had shut the heavy wood door which locks instantly and was basically inescapable for an animal. She knew she would have to let him out. *Damn!* she said, as she tried to think of how she would be able to open the door without coming in harm's way. *He's had two opportunities to attack me. He's not as menacing as he looks,* she thought. Giselle got up off the couch and opened her sliding back door and opened the screen. She could hear him whimper. "Ok. I have to let him out. But wait," she said, as she tried to think of the best way to free it without getting to close. "I know what. I'll take my shotgun. I just won't point it at him, but I'll be ready. I'll have to keep my distance if I want to hit him."

Giselle walked to the shed slowly, with her shotgun in hand and so nervous that she was trembling. "How the hell am I going to hit anything with my hands shaking. Calm down Giselle," she said to herself, pausing then continuing on. She held the shotgun down to her side and then quickly open the door and ran back, ready to aim. She watched the door waiting for him to exit and was becoming more and more nervous. After a few minutes, the wolf walked out slowly and walked slowly passed Giselle and toward her house. "No, no, no. Where are you going," she said, as the animal walked right through her open door and into her house. "Fuck... Great... Now he's in my house."

Fear set in as she approached the door. Giselle walked in slowly and saw the animal was laying on her shaggy throw in front of her fire place. "I thought they were afraid of fire. This is definitely someone's pet," she stated as she walked closer. "Come on go. Shu. Go on. Get outta here," she said, in an effort to get the massively large animal out of her house. After trying for twenty minutes to get the animal to leave, Giselle decided she would let it stay. She sighed then went and got him a bowl of water and sat it near the door. She didn't want to trap him inside so she decided to leave the door slightly ajar. "Ok. I hope you can kill a bear because if one gets in here, you're on your own. I'll be safe in my room with the door closed and a shotgun by my side."

Giselle went to her room and closed her door and leaned the gun against the wall. *That's someone's pet. I didn't know you could domesticate a wolf living in the wild. They must have had it since it was a puppy,* she thought, as she sat on her bed. "Damn! I still have one more thing to add to my report. Ok. So, I guess I'll have to get up at five."

Giselle got in the shower and took her time as she relaxed under the warm water. She rubbed soap into her washcloth and lathered her body. She thought of her wild weekend that showed no signs of letting up. But in all the chaos, she had become less afraid of the wolf that was currently resting on her favorite throw rug. The animal that vehemently fought to protect her and then escorted her home like a personal body guard. *Unbelievable!* she thought, as she exited the shower and put her pajama's on. She set her alarm clock for five in the morning and pulled the covers up. She hoped to get enough rest so she would be focused and able to complete her work in the morning.

Visions of the wolf and a man came to her in her dreams. Giselle tossed and turned and moaned, as visions of a black wolf chasing her, had her gripped in fear. She kicked her legs as her dream showed her running through trees. She ran into a clearing where other wolves were but ran swiftly past them. The all black wolf with a patch of white hair on its nose kept close behind her. When she looked back, it was a man chasing her. Giselle jolted awake, breathing heavily and looking around. "What? What kind of dream was that? The wolf turned into the guy from the coffee shop. And who is Alonzo? Where did I get that name from?" she said, as she got up and opened her sliding door slightly. She needed fresh air.

It was the middle of the night and stars were shining brightly in the sky. Giselle looked at the clock. It was one o'clock in the morning. She sat on the bed staring into the darkness. Her dream seemed real. Vivid. She thought about the man. Then she thought about the wolf. Memories from her childhood came to mind. She remembered the huge black wolf with a white patch on its nose. Her eyes got big. It couldn't be. Giselle focused on her memories as she tried to picture everything about the wolf from her past. "That's the wolf from when I was a child? But that's impossible. He would probably be dead now. Wolves don't live twenty years. Maybe that wolf is related. He has the same patch? But why are they drawn to me. Why do I keep coming into contact with black wolves with a white patch? This is just weird. Somethings not right," she said, as she reflected on her dream. Giselle was trying to piece the strange occurrences together. She had no idea how the puzzle fit together, but she had every intention of finding out.

At three in the morning, Giselle rose and slowly opened her door and walked carefully and slowly down her hall. She looked down the staircase and could see the wolf laying closer to her stairs as if he was keeping watch. Giselle sighed. She hoped he would be gone. She slowly walked down the stairs trying not to wake it and then tried to ease past him when she got to the bottom step. The wolf raised up, looked at her then laid his head back down. Giselle paused then walked softly in the kitchen constantly looking back and grabbed her laptop then walked back.

Please don't move, she thought, as she neared him. Giselle eased past him and went slowly up the stairs picking up the pace when she got to the top and rushed to her room. She shut the door then took a deep breath. She was still cautious of the oversized wolf that could kill her in just a matter of seconds. She was raised with animals all her life. She'd had a dog throughout her childhood and into her adult years and was good at picking up cues from animals. But the black wolf that seemed harmless was hard to read. She felt safe, but there was something about it that wasn't domesticated.

"Yes. Done," she said, stretching her arms and then reaching over and setting her alarm clock. She had three and a half hours before she needed to get up and she closed her eyes, falling fast asleep.

Giselle fell into a deep sleep and had dreams of wolves running around and a man standing with a pack in the forest. She tossed and turned and moaned as she dreamed and reacted to visions of a man kissing and touching her. She moved her head side to side as the man touched her lightly, sending chills through her body.

Giselle moaned as he kissed and touched her all over. His touch made her want him. She pulled him closer and wrapped her legs around him. "Alonzo," she whispered then kissed his ear. "I love you," she said softly. He turned his head towards her and buried it deep in her neck as he entered her. Giselle screamed with delight as she felt him enter her. She closed her eyes and rubbed her nails up his back as he made love to her. Her body felt intense sensations she had never experienced.

She moved her body against his, as she was hungry for more of him. I love you Giselle," he said, as he kissed her passionately. He looked into her eyes, and Giselle watched as his eyes turned into a vibrant reddish-brown color. Her emotions about what she was feeling engulfed her. She shed a tear which he kissed away, then asked her why she was crying. Giselle stared at him. She felt overwhelmed. As he started to kiss her gently on her eye then down to her lips and Giselle awoke.

"What?" she said, confused and looking around. She removed her hands from inside her panties and sat up. She had never had a dream that vivid before. She moved her hair from her face and tucked it behind her ears. Breathing at a fast pace and still feeling the effects of a powerful orgasm, Giselle looked around, confused. Her body felt as though she'd had sex. Her vagina had a throbbing intensity. She felt touched all over. Not one inch of her body was hers. It felt as though it belonged to someone else for a moment. As though she had been possessed. She jumped up from her bed alert and wondering how the dream felt so real. How was it that it felt so good.

Giselle got out of bed and went into her bathroom. "What is happening," she said, as she rubbed her head in confusion. She was still breathing heavily as she tried again, to focus on her visions. "The same dream. Him again. In my dream. Again," she said, as she tried to calm herself. It was quiet and peaceful and she had just another hour before she would need to get ready for work. She put water in a cup and drank it. "Wow. That was vivid," she said, as she closed her eyes and pictured the events of the wet dream she'd had.

She walked back into her room and over to her door. She walked down the hall and stood at the top of the stairs. To her surprise the wolf was gone. "Where did he go," she said, as she walked down the steps slowly and went to the door. *Wait! I left this open!* Giselle grew concerned, thinking someone had possibly been in her home. She grabbed her gun and looked room to room and in every closet until she cleared the entire house. *What the hell! Wolves close doors now!*

Giselle tried to return to sleep but was unable to. She made herself eggs and toast and decided to stay awake until it was time to leave out. After eating, she returned to her room and sat on her bed. The sun was rising above the lake and cast a red light on the water. She walked over to her large uncovered window and out at the trees. She glanced over at the lake that was in the distance. She loved her view. She loved the home that she grew up in and now owned. Many people had tried to buy it from her but no amount of compensation was worth what she was looking at.

Every time she looked towards the woods, it evoked comfortable feelings of warmth and familiarity. A longing. Something about it was mysterious, breathtaking and captivating. She stared in the distance and thought she saw wolves. More than one, walking around. She walked quickly to her office to grab her binoculars and came back and scanned the trees but could no longer see them. She sighed then hurried and looked again as she saw a figure moving near the pine trees.

Giselle gasped when she saw a wolf emerge from forest. It wasn't the one that had made itself her guest for the night and wasn't as large, but was still larger than any wolf she'd seen. "These wolves are large," she said, as she dropped the binoculars from her eyes and walked away. At peace and feeling something similar to love and protection, she walked away from the window and retreated into her bathroom. Unaware that Alonzo, the man in her dreams, was watching from a tree.

Grant drove through town, on his way to one of their satellite offices nestled near the border between Kamiah and the next town. It sat on the edge of town, near trees that occupied the rest of the land heading north. The town had a picturesque view of endless mountains and trees and was the reason it was gaining in popularity. The reason behind the rush of new residents to Kamiah and its neighboring towns. "How you doing Sheriff," the man said, as he passed Grant. "Hey Tom," he replied.

Grant was a handsome, athletically built thirty two year old man who came from a long line of men in law enforcement. Grant took his job seriously as did his father and his grandfather. He was one of the few African American men residing in the small, quaint and booming town that was growing in diversity as well as wealth. "Marguerite. Anything exciting happen while I was out," he asked, smiling at the secretary who had worked for the Kamiah Sheriff's Office for years. She was the wife of his good friend Mack. And was loyal and hardworking. He depended on her and she never let him down.

"Another sighting of a large wolf. They say it's massive. Possibly as large as seven feet, maybe two hundred and fifty pounds," Marguerite said. "Wolves aren't that big. The largest wolf ever recorded was six feet," Grant replied. "I know. But Mr. Holmes is no stranger to wolves. He knows them inside and out. That's what he said. He wants you to come by and talk to him. He shot at it but missed. Said we need to spend a few days and hunt it and its pack. He's sure it's an alpha. He said he saw two of them together." Grant walked over to his files and then got on his computer. "Call him and tell him I'll be by later today. Tell him don't worry. We'll get more proactive. We'll hunt them down and kill them."

"This is great Giselle. Fine work. Perfect!" Mr. Garner said, as he reviewed the spreadsheet with pride. He wasn't really worried. He had faith in Giselle. She had always come through on even the toughest of assignments. It was why her power at the company was steadily growing and why Mr. Garner was considering her for partner. Giselle smiled and stood there making sure he reviewed the spreadsheet thoroughly. She wanted to run and grab something to eat, but didn't want to be out of the office in case he had a change. As she stood there, she began to feel hot and tense. It was feelings of sexual intensity and she stood there puzzled as to its sudden onset when her mind was not on anything of a sexual nature.

What the hell is wrong with you? she thought to herself, as she stood at Mr. Garner desk. "I don't have any changes. Thanks. Will you be sitting in on this one?" Mr. Garner asked. "No. Unless you want me there. I have other things I need to get started on," she replied. "No. I can handle him. He's a tiger but I'm a shark. I'll get that account for sure. He's tough but he doesn't know I have a secret weapon," he bragged, referring to her. Giselle smiled and walked out of his office as he picked up the phone to make a call. She walked slowly to her office, next door to his and over to the window. She rubbed her neck and closed her eyes. She was still feeling aroused and wanted it to end. She had no way to quench her desires and she was in the middle of a long day. She had already anticipated being at work past closing time. But the intensity of what she was feeling, was hindering those plans.

She walked over to her desk and grabbed her cell phone and called Grant. "Hey," he answered. "Hey. What you doing?" she asked. "Nothing baby. What you up to?" he asked, as he read through a case. "Nothing," she said, holding the phone and walking back over to the window and looking down at the towns people walking the streets. "Ok. You want something. I can tell. The answer is yes to whatever it is," he said. Giselle smiled. "I haven't even asked you yet," she replied. Grant smiled. "Well yes anyway," he said.

Giselle continued to look at the pedestrians as they walked around on the streets and suddenly felt the feeling she was having, leave, just as quickly as it came. "Nothing. I was just calling to see what you were doing. I did want to see you later but I just realized I have work to do," she said, as she looked out and noticed a man standing and appearing to be focused on her. He was too far away to see clearly, but Giselle felt he was looking at her. *Is that the same guy*, she thought as she held the phone. "I want to see you Giselle. You never want to see me anymore. I can still come by. I can come when you leave there and go home. Whatever time that is," he pleaded. He missed her and was trying to stay strong and allow her to reach out to him. Giselle was the type of woman that needed her space and would shut down if she felt harassed or too heavily pursued. "Ok. I'll call you when I leave," she said, hanging up and watching as the man turned and walked away. She watched as he bent the corner and walked out of view. *Was that him. The man from the coffee shop?*

Giselle had a long day and was fatigued. She sat back in her chair and took a deep breath then picked up her phone to check missed calls and texts. Her mind drifted to her brief and intense feelings from earlier in the day. She wondered why those feelings had not returned. Usually when her desires fired up that intensely, only sex would take the feeling away. She would need to get physical in order to be satisfied and quench her desires. But the feeling didn't return. Giselle hoped Grant would be too tired to come over. There was no getting away from him if he thought she was horny and wanting him. He would worry that another man would be there to satisfy her and the thought would surely drive him insane.

After a few hours, Giselle was ready to go. She looked at her phone and sighed as she read a text from Grant; *Call me when you leave. I miss you. I'm at your house trimming trees. I'm almost done. Hit me back if you want me to wait on you. Otherwise, I can go home and shower and wait on your call.* Giselle sat her phone down. Grant was being Grant again. Trying to make himself useful and showing up unannounced hoping to be with her. She cared for him and hoped he would have met someone and directed some of the unwanted attention their way. But Grant was in love and he would not be deterred.

Grant was working hard in the late afternoon sun, cutting down a few trees for Giselle to use in her fire place. He had scaled back some of the branches on some of the surrounding trees. And he planned on having the grass cut by the time she got home. Grant stood over the self-made table he constructed and chopped the wood, as he wiped his head and took short breaks. "Damn it's hot out here," he complained, as he swung the axe, slicing the wood in half. He looked rugged yet handsome in his Levi 501 jeans and a navy blue tee.

The sun was constant and with very little clouds in the sky, he began to feel fatigued from the heat. Grant took a few gulps from his water and sat it back down and wiped his forehead again before taking the axe over his head and coming down with great force. "Uh," he grunted, as he swung the axe again. His grunts were loud and echoed through the air, resonating into the distance and catching the attention of an unknown rival.

Chapter Four - Blackwolf

Blackwolf stood over his kill looking at his hungry pack that relied heavily on him. He could bring down a 700 pound Elk with ease and in a matter of seconds. The pack had migrated deeper into the woods, as they followed Blackwolf on a journey. They needed to get further away from human civilization and further away from the plan to annihilate the wolves. Blackwolf was aware of the kill order and was protecting his pack from two separate enemies. A rival pack of large grey wolves lead by another shifter, his cousin named Darius. And their human enemy, a group of men being led by his new rival, Grant.

Blackwolf himself was a shifter who changed under the night of the full moon and would return to man form by dawn. But the Curse of the Indies, from an Indian witch name Kakia, cursed his family as the witch vowed to make them suffer for their crimes. She placed a 361 lunar cycle curse on all first born males of the Andino family. The only way to break the curse was the true love of a woman before their 30th birthday. If the male had no mate or female that loved him by the 361st moon after his birth, he would remain a wolf for 300 years or until killed by a silver bullet through the heart. Kakia lost her entire tribal family at the hands of the sons of the Andino family and she vowed revenge.

But the Andino family had powers within their own family. They hailed their elder great aunts as the greatest witches and brew queens that ever lived. The Andino women, although unsuccessful with removing the curse, conjured up ways for the men to use the curse for their own needs. They would have the ability to shift by choice. And the men were given special powers to enhance their attraction to the opposite sex and were made more virile. The first-born male would also have super human strength when in man form and be more powerful than any animal when in wolf form. They would have high frequency range of sound and vision capable of seeing objects over a mile away. With their sight being best at night. Their most notable and important abilities would be that of telepathy and channeling. If the first born male Andino marked a young girl or woman while in wolf form, he would have telepathic abilities with her and be able to hear her thoughts as if she was speaking to him. They would also have the ability to channel the woman physically to increase the attraction between them.

With these changes, the Andino women were able to soften the blow of the curse and improve the Andino males' chances of survival. And help in breaking the *Curse of Indie.* And as time went on, hundreds of years later, the curse remained. But the changes that occurred enhanced even more and the first born males fine tuned their abilities and learned to adapt to both worlds. By the time Alonzo was born to an African mother named Mirra and European father named Alexander Andino, he bore the curse as he was his father's first-born son.

Alonzo walked away, allowing the pack to feast on his kill and laid down near a tree. He only came to the forest to check on the members and make sure they had plenty to eat. He'd lived amongst them since he was a newborn. Introduced to the pack by an alpha female wolf who raised him as her own. And this was the only family he knew. He never knew his father who had been killed by a rival. His own cousin, who wanted to eliminate him because of their love for the same woman. Alonzo's mother Mirra. The cousins were both in love with her but Nikos' charm and slick words lured Mirra into his fold. She soon fell in love with him and by age thirty, it became painfully obvious who she loved. Nikos Andino no longer changed at the full moon. It was proof of Mirra's love for him as the curse had been broken. But what was added by their aunts centuries ago, remained. He still had the ability to change into a wolf but only if he wanted.

Nikos was a few years older than Alexander. Alexander still had time to break his curse. But in order to keep his secret, and out of jealousy over Mirra, Nikos killed Alonzo's father Alexander. He killed him prior to his last moon, in fear that Alonzo's mother Mirra would fall in love with him and to keep him quiet. He never realized that she only loved him and that his act of cruelty was in vain. After Nikos killed Alexander, he forced Mirra to throw his son, Alonzo, into the forest. Alonzo, cast into shrubs deep within the forest, turned into a baby pup at the first moon after his birth. He was only a few days old when he changed. A female alpha wolf who had just given birth, found him and adopted him. He stayed in the forest with the pack in wolf form, until he was ten years old.

Alonzo grew into a superbly strong wolf, capable of overtaking all that came up against him. He smelled the scent of his enemy when Nikos tossed him in the forest. And when he became a man, he hunted the scent down and killed him. Now

Nikos' son Darius sought to even the score and wanted to kill Alonzo. But Alonzo was stronger than him and so he started taking out Alonzo's pack, one by one, just to hurt him and destroy the only family he knew. The pack was all Alonzo had and was the sole reason he changed, by choice, into a wolf. He stayed in wolf form in order to protect the pack from Darius and his much bigger and stronger pack. Both he and Darius were the only wolf shifters in their packs and they resided over the packs as alpha males protecting and controlling the members. Darius had more beta males than Alonzo and had them killing the towns livestock hoping Alonzo's pack would be blamed for it forcing the men to hunt Alonzo and his pack and kill them all.

Darius was thirty one and was already cursed to remain a wolf. He never found true love and so he would never be able to shift into a man ever again. He resented this and harbored jealousy and resentment towards Alonzo. Alonzo was only twenty eight and still had two years to meet and fall in love with a woman. Alonzo had already marked the woman he loved. He'd loved her since they were ten years old when her father pointed a gun at him.

He licked her face while he had a rare moment in her presence, forever marking her. He marked Giselle that day and watched her from trees and through shrubs. Until the fateful day her father moved the family to Canada. Once Giselle crossed the water, her scent was lost and he was unable to track her.

Giselle had returned to Idaho to claim her childhood home. To return to the place that held all her fond memories. But something else drew her back. A force more powerful than the property she grew up in. She didn't know what it was but Alonzo knew. She was back and she was his. He just had to figure a way to get her to fall in love with the man form of himself. He had befriended her in wolf form. But the curse would only be broken if it was true love, consummated before 361 lunar cycles.

Grant was chopping wood and stacking it against Giselle's home, waiting for her to return from work. He had done work on her house and knew secret ways to gain access to her home from outside. She was unaware that two of her windows had weak points and could be manipulated and opened. Grant looked out into the wilderness and thought he saw something in the distance. He squinted his eyes as he strained to see what it was. He continued gathering the wood and placing it in a neat pile. The forest had all sorts of wildlife. Grant thought nothing more of the movement through the vegetation.

Grant was tired and ready to quit chopping wood for the day. He kneeled down to grab the last few pieces then stood up and froze. He slowly turned around and looked in horror as a massive, all black wolf slowly approached. The wolf growled and lowered his body in an attack stance. Grant slowly released the wood. But held on to one piece. He took a few steps back and looked around. Giselle had no neighbors. Grant knew he was in a bad position. "Ok boy. Ok," he said, as he continued to back up. Grant could not believe his eyes. The animal was larger than anything they had on record and he was no match for it. Just as the animal got closer Giselle bent the corner.

"No," she shouted, as she ran up to the wolf. "Giselle. Get back!" grant shouted, as he took a few more steps back. The wolf continued his approach and Giselle stood in front of him and reached her hand out. Grant ran to his truck, sweating and nervous as he feared for his and Giselle's life. The animal looked at her and she stared back at him. She shook her head no and touched its nose. The wolf licked her hand, turned and ran through the grass, through the dense vegetation and into the forest.

Grant opened the door to his F150 and grabbed a rifle and chased the animal into the forest.

"Grant no," Giselle said, as she ran behind him. Grant could see the back of the animal and aimed his high-powered rifle at it and took a shot. "I think I hit him. Damn! He's still running though. He'll probably collapse at some point. I'm going through that forest Giselle and see if I got him. That thing was massive," he said, walked briskly towards his truck. "Grant. Its gone. What are you doing?" she asked, worried about the wolf. "Did you see that thing? So that's what's been killing all the large livestock. That thing had been killing everything including Bison," he cautioned.

"No Grant. He's not vicious. You're not killing that animal on my property. We talked about this. That wolf saved me from another wolf attack," she said. "What! Why would it do that Giselle. Wild wolves aren't domesticated like that. He has no instinct to protect humans. A full grown wolf is not going to befriend you and protect you the way your dog would. That's just absurd," he said. "Yes it did. Didn't you see it lick my hand. It walked home with me. It did. And you're not killing it." Grant looked at her and looked back into the forest. "That thing has to be stopped. It growled at me. If you hadn't come along, I'd be dead. Eaten. That thing was about to attack. I would have been killed Giselle. Do you understand. I have to protect the people and their livestock. I'll be back tomorrow with my men," he said. "Don't do this Grant," she pleaded. "Stay out of it Giselle. Let me do my job."

Giselle turned away and walked into her home, slamming the door shut. Grant got in his truck and radioed the Sheriff's office. "Marguerite. You there," he said into the walkie talkie. "Yes Sheriff Ellis," she radioed back. "I want you to call in some of the deputies. Call anyone we can get who's hunted wolves before and anyone in town who can help. I spotted that wolf that's been killing off livestock and we have to go in the forest after it. It's over here near Berry Road in the Wallowa Forest," he said. "Will do Sheriff."

Grant looked back at Giselle and they locked eyes before she walked away from the window. Grant was torn. He picked up his phone and called her, but she didn't answer. *Damn!* he said, getting out of the car and walking up to her door. Grant didn't want her mad at him. But he was more determined to kill the wolf that he felt was unpredictable and could attack without cause. Possibly kill the woman he loved. Grant stood at her door and thought about knocking. He raised his hand then paused. Grant turned and walked back to his car and looked once again before pulling off. *She just needs time to cool off,* he thought, as he drove away.

Alonzo stood three hundred feet away in the distance nears the trees. He stared at Giselle as she walked through her house with a cup of tea. He watched her walk into her great room and plop down on her couch. She sat with her legs folded looking out into the wilderness. He had keen and powerful vision that could see from hundreds of feet away in great detail. He watched as her eyes showed a blank stare. She appeared bothered. He could hear her thoughts and tuned in to what she was thinking. It was about him. It involved his wolf family. The pack. She was afraid for him. For Blackwolf. The man he had started to hate and was about to attack, wanted him dead. The man who was standing in his way of his one true mate, was planning to kill him or any wolf found within in the area. Alonzo turned and walked away. He needed to migrate the wolves deeper in the forest and then hunt down his enemy. He had two enemies but one was the biggest threat of all. Grant was now enemy number one.

Alonzo ran through the forest on foot at speeds of nearly 90 mph then slowed and changed into *Blackwolf*. His spiritual name given to him by a member of the Shieu Tribe. A gentleman by the name of Ahanu, when he saved his life from an attack by a Kodiak bear near Granite Lake. Blackwolf's speed was over 100 mph with precision as his keen sight foresaw all obstacles before he reached them. Allowing him to cut through the forest like a knife. Blackwolf ran for three miles until he reached the fork of the Salmon River.

He found his pack and walked through slowly as the beta and omega wolves lowered their heads in submission. The pack hadn't seen Blackwolf in days. They had been successful on their own hunting Elk and sticking close to the river for water. Blackwolf noticed one of the larger beta wolves was missing. It was easily recognized as it was grey with a distinctive dark grey patch on its chest. Blackwolf suddenly smelled the foul odor of decay and ran back through the forest towards the scent. He went downriver and through a large pine tree area until he came upon the carcass. The body was intact except for a large hole in its abdomen.

Just as he stood over it mourning the death of his family member a shot rang out in the distance. Blackwolf looked around and could see a group of men on three-wheelers coming his way. He took off running hoping he could get to his pack before they did, shots continued to ring out as the men tried to catch the wolf. They didn't have much open plains to drive on before they would have to abandon the three wheelers and travel on foot. That would be daunting and could get dangerous if night fell. Wallowa was filled with bears, wolves and mountain lions. The forest was responsible for several deaths a year attributed to animal attacks.

Blackwolf ran and looked back. The men were still in pursuit. One of the men in pursuit was Grant. He had assembled a small team to kill the wolves and recognized the all black wolf with a white patch. He stopped his four-wheel ATV and looked through his high-powered scope and took the shot. He saw the wolf stumble then continue running. "I got it," he said, as the men began driving again in the direction of the wolf. When they reached the area, the black wolf was nowhere in sight which puzzled Grant. He had special *Black Talon* bullets designed to rip anything it penetrated with precision and tremendous force. He had clear line to sight and was sure the bullet went into the animals back.

"Grant. We see nothing. You sure you hit it. There's nothing," deputy Clark Anderson said over the walkie talkie. "Keep checking. Spread out. I'm sure I hit it," Grant replied. Grant drove around, going deeper into the forest hoping to find either a wounded or a dead wolf. He had a personal vendetta against the wolf he was sure, was the same one that nearly attacked him outside of Giselle's home. "Grant," his deputy radioed. "Yeah," he replied. "Listen. We're still not finding anything and it's getting dark. Let's call it for now and come back tomorrow." Grant hesitated. He wanted that wolf dead. Wolves were smart and if they felt as though their territory had been encroached by humans, the pack would move on. Grant paused. "We still have an hour," he said.

His deputy sighed. The men around him shook their head no. No one thought it was safe to continue as dusk would be approaching. They whispered to each other their fears when they saw the size of the wolf they were pursuing. None of them had ever seen a wolf that size and feared the whole pack may be just as large. Which could mean harder to kill. Only Grant had the Black Talon bullets and the other men were ready to go. They vowed not to return. It didn't feel right. There were rumors of spirits in the woods protecting the wolves. "Hey. Listen man. That was no regular wolf. That might be Blackwolf. The wolf that saved the Sheiu elder who was at the river being attacked by a bear. His relatives will tell you all about the *Legend of Blackwolf*. Legend has it he's immortal and only a silver bullet will kill him. I'm not risking my life for no wolf that can't be killed and we have no silver bullets. A group of men years ago went after it because they were losing their house pets and livestock and no one ever seen or heard from them again."

Deputy Anderson looked around and then got back on his walkie talkie. "Grant. No one wants to stay. It's too risky. Let's just go for now and come back in the morning," he said, then turned his attention to the nervous and unsure hunter. "That just old wives' tales. I heard about the legend. First off, a single wolf cannot beat a full-grown Kodiak bear. Secondly, if it were true, wolves don't live twenty five years so that wouldn't be the same wolf. And that's hogwash that the bullet has to be silver. Grant has one of the most powerful bullets made. But I do agree that we should leave for the evening and return at sun up."

Grant drove back toward where the group of men were and they headed back to their cars. They placed the three and four wheelers on dollies and secured the vehicles for transport. "Hey Grant. Tom was saying the wolf you shot was rumored to be indestructible. You ever heard of the legend of Blackwolf?" he asked. "Yeah. Who hasn't. It's a bunch of crap. It's an old legend that no one ever disputed and so no one ever came forward with any proof. It was centered around the Sheiu Tribe members and their belief that they were being protected by spirits. Spirits that could appear in wolf form. When one of the elders was saved by a wolf, it solidified their belief in the myth and it still means something to them to this day. I don't believe in myths. They are nothing more than coincidences. Period," Grant said, as he hooked the ATV to the Dollie. "I still want you to assemble the best crew you can so we can get back out here tomorrow and kills these wolves," he added as he walked towards his truck.

Giselle walked through her large home, lighting a few candles and relaxing to soft music. Unaware that Grant had started his wolf hunt in the forest just beyond her home. She looked up into the night sky and admired the full and bright moon as it shone over her home. She admired the trees outlining the forest in the distance. Her eyes scanned the ground then stopped when she saw movement. Something near the lake. She could see a shadowy figure near the edge of the water but she couldn't make out what the large object was. She stared for a few minutes then went to her closet to retrieve her shotgun, just in case. Giselle went back to the window and saw the figure was gone. She walked away and went into her kitchen, searching for a late-night snack. She sighed when she could not settle on anything in particular and decided to go get a pizza.

Chapter Five - Shots Fired

It was an unusually cold evening. Giselle walked up to her car looking around before she got in. The sighting of something near the lake had her slightly on edge. "It's chilly out here tonight," she said, as she walked to her Jeep and got in. *I'm not feeling this at all but I'm hungry. Maybe I should make oatmeal and call it a night,* she contemplated, as she sat there thinking. "Oh well. I'm going," she said, as she started the car and pulled off. She took her time driving down the unleveled gravel drive. She had her friends at the Idaho Road Commission put in an order to street sweep her private road and remove the rocks. Then come in with dirt and sand and level it. She blamed the rocks for the flat tires she'd gotten over the years. And didn't want to take any chances in the near future.

"Ok. This will be quick," she said, as she pulled off. Something was in the road up ahead. When she got closer she gasped, then slammed on the breaks. Her headlights were shinning on a man lying in the middle of her road. Giselle looked around. "What the hell," she said. She reached for her phone to call Grant and sighed when he didn't answer. Giselle's had a good friend named Ming, who was an accomplished surgeon and writer. She called her to get advice on whether to try moving the man. He lay motionless in the middle of her road and she wasn't sure what she should do. Giselle decided to check him first. Maybe he was intoxicated and had fallen asleep. Maybe he was sick and needed help.

"Hi this is Dr. Lee," she answered. "Ming. I'm so glad you answered. I have an emergency. There's a man in my driveway. He's not moving. How do I perform first aid? I have no idea what to do," she said. "Oh my GiGi. I can send an ambulance," Ming replied. "They take forever to get out this way so it's not a number I think to use. I tried calling Grant already. I will see if I can get him to the hospital. I have to get him out the road before the smell of his blood brings unwanted guest. I see a little blood on his shirt," she said cautiously. "Put me on speaker phone and then go slowly over to him. Did you look around. Be safe GiGi," Ming advised. "I have my gun in the glove compartment," she replied, reaching for it before opening her car door.

Giselle walked slowly, looking around and holding on to the handle of the gun. As she got closer, she recognized the man. He was the handsome stranger who she'd seen around town and at the coffee shop. The man who had started appearing in her dreams. Giselle rushed to his side and turned him over. He was breathing but appeared to be unconscious. "Sir… Hey," she said, as she shook him. Giselle ran back to her car and grabbed a blanket and rolled him on top of it then pulled him to her car.

He was heavy, but she managed to pull him successfully to the back of the car and open the door. She stood there trying to figure out how she would get him inside the car when she heard wolves howling. "Shit," she blurted and then shook him. "Help me get you up," she said, as she pulled him by the shirt and got him on his knees, leaning his top half inside the door. She then pushed his back and he crawled into the car then collapsed again. Giselle shut the door and turned her car around and went back to the house. She grabbed her phone and called Grant again but got no answer. "Now he's unavailable," she complained, as she pulled up to her house and used her garage door opener to open one of the doors. She had a three-car attached garage that she never parked in, but the howling sounds were getting closer and she needed to be inside.

Giselle tried to wake him but he was out cold. She pulled him by his legs and when she had him in position, she pulled his arms, pulling him out of the car. "Oh shoot. I'm sorry," she said, as his body hit the floor. Giselle got him back on the comforter and proceeded to pull him into her house. "Ok. Let me call Ming back," she said, realizing she'd lost the call. "Hey. What happened? I see you're still alive. Where's the man?" Ming asked. "Well. Right now, he's on the kitchen floor," she replied.

"What! GiGi! No! You have a stranger on your kitchen floor. What if he comes to, rapes and kills you," she warned. "Ming. He's been shot. I pulled his shirt up. He has a bullet whole," she said. "Ok. Well he definitely needs to be in the hospital then. Call *City One Ambulance* and they'll be there. They are the closest to where you stay." Giselle got down on her knees and close to his face. "He's breathing. I don't see a lot of blood. I think he's going to be ok. I'll call them and call you back," she replied.

Giselle paced the floor. She didn't think they'd come quick enough and she didn't want anything to happen to the handsome stranger who had caught her attention on more than one occasion. Giselle did an internet search to pull up the ambulance's phone number. "Hi where's your emergency," the operator said. "Um yes. I have an injured man on my floor. Can you send an ambulance?" she said, pacing the floor. "Ok. Mam. Can you tell me what's wrong with him?" the operator asked. "Well. It looks like a bullet hole in his back but I don't know for sure," she said. "Ok. Mam. What's the address?" the operator asked. "Hang up. I'm not going to no hospital," the man said, still laying on her floor with his eyes closed.

Giselle was startled and jumped from nerves and shock.

"Um. Wait. He just spoke. He says he's fine. He doesn't want an ambulance," she said. "Ok. What? So is he shot or not because he will need medical attention if he's been shot. It's possible he doesn't know what he's saying due to blood loss and shock. We will need to come and access him. Can you please give us the address?" the operator asked. "No. Hang up," he answered. Giselle was shocked he knew what was being said. She didn't have the call on speaker and she was far enough away from him that he wouldn't have been able to hear the person on the other end of the line. "Giselle pushed mute on her phone. "Are you sure you don't want to go. You have a hole in your back," she warned. "No. I don't want to go," he replied. Giselle hung up and her phone immediately rang. "It's them calling back," she said. "Answer and tell them I've gone," he replied

Giselle helped Alonzo to her couch and he laid down. "What's your name?" she asked the stranger. "Alonzo," he replied. Giselle was shocked when he said his name. It was the name she whispered in her dreams. The name that belonged to a face she never fully saw. Just the eyes. The reddish brown eyes that glowed. "What happened to you?" she asked, kneeling in front of him. Alonzo didn't answer as he lay there appearing to nod off. He didn't look to be in much pain but Giselle was concerned because his movements were slow and deliberate. "Listen. I need you to pull the bullet out my back," he said, looking directly in her eyes for the first time and appearing unfazed by the serious nature of his request. "You want me to pull a bullet out of your back. I have no medical tools here. I could hit an artery. You could catch an infection. I could push it in further and do more damage. That doesn't sound like a good idea," she cautioned.

"It's at the surface. All you need is tweezers," he said. "What! Wait. How do you know where it is?" she asked. "I felt it," he replied quickly, realizing that he didn't need to give her more reason for skepticism. The injury was in a spot he would have had a hard time reaching but Giselle didn't want to continually question him so she left it alone. "I'll try ok. I have to go get my tweezers," she said, as she hurried to her bathroom. "Make sure you burn them first," he shouted.

"What are you doing Gi. You're going to get a bullet out of his back. What is happening," she said, as she searched her cabinet. Giselle cleaned her tweezers with alcohol then burned the tips and sat them in a bowl. She grabbed her vinegar, hydrogen peroxide and alcohol and took it to her living room. She ran back and got white towels and a needle and thread. As she set up her items, preparing for the extraction, she looked at him. She was surprised at the level of comfort she felt. As if they knew one another. She couldn't help to think that they were fated to meet. Between what the barista at the coffee shop had told her and what Grant had said, she felt as though they were supposed to meet. Just not under these circumstances.

His eyes were closed and he looked too comfortable for a man about to endure unbearable pain. The type of pain he would surely be feeling as an unexperienced, untrained person tried to mimic what they saw on Grey's Anatomy. But nonetheless, Giselle was fearless. She was just the sort of woman who would be strong enough to attempt such a feat. She held the tweezer then took a deep breath. "Turn over," she said. Alonzo stared at her briefly then gave her a smile. Giselle smiled back at him and he raised up to remove his shirt. Alonzo pulled his tee shirt over his head and turned over on his stomach. Giselle couldn't help but admire his well-toned physique. "I want to apologize in advance if this hurts. I'm not a nurse," she said. "You're fine," he said, with his face turned in the opposite direction. Giselle froze up and he turned to look at her. "It's ok," he said, flashing the handsome smile that she thought was the sexiest smile on the planet.

She instantly relaxed and began wiping the area clean. She touched the hole. She was curious about the lack of blood surrounding it. "Ok. This is gonna hurt," she said, as she went into the hole, which was the size of a nickel and pulled out the bullet. She placed it in the bowl and looked at the hole in his back. His wound seemed so superficial, that she questioned what type of gun was used. Even a 22 would have resulted in a bullet being deeper inside the flesh. Giselle was impressed. He didn't make one sound. No moan. No groan. No yelling out in pain. Nothing. "Ok. It's out. What now," she asked. "Nothing. You have a Band-Aid," he asked.

"Band-Aid! Over a hole. You have to close this up. It will get infected," she warned. "It'll be fine. Just put a Band-Aid on it," he said, with his eyes closed, appearing to be falling back asleep. Giselle sat there on her knees staring at him. She looked him over. His muscles. His perfect skin. His sexy thick eyebrows, mustache, goatee and beard. Perfectly cut and trimmed. Her senses keyed into the smell of his cologne and the fact that visually, he was turning her on. He seemed to be sleeping liking a baby and she was glad that she was able to help him. She wanted to know him. Know all about him. Where he was from. Where he worked. Whether he was married and had family. And what happened that resulted in him being shot in the back.

But her questions would have to wait. She felt comfortable allowing him to stay on her couch. His presence seemed familiar. Like he had been there before. His smell was familiar and she swore she'd smelled him before. In a more up close and personal way. Giselle sat there for a few minutes before getting up and disposing of everything. She kept the bullet inside of the small bowl. She put her cleaning items away and then cut the lamp off on her table near the couch where he slept. *Ok. What now. I have a stranger asleep in my house. Why do strange things keep happening to me? What kind of life is this I'm living,* she thought, as she walked up her stairs and into her bedroom and closed her door.

Giselle sat on the edge of her bed still puzzled as to why his presence in her home felt right and normal. *I don't know him. Not from school, or college or work. Other than seeing him at the coffee shop, I don't know him,* she thought, as she looked off, staring at the wall. *I have to get some sleep. This has been yet another crazy evening.*

Giselle laid down and pulled the sheets up and looked over at her door. She felt a warm sensation come over her. She took a deep breath and laid there, kicking the covers off believing it was the source of heat she was feeling. Giselle turned on her side and stared at her door. She wondered if her new house guest had woken up. There was a part of her that wanted to go check but she decided against it and closed her eyes, immediately falling into a deep sleep.

The cool night air came in through a small crack in her window. Giselle was restless and moved around in her bed. She turned on her back then over to her left side and then back to her right. She tossed and turned as images of a dark skinned, man whose face she couldn't see touched her hair and pulled her close to him. It was dark and all she could see were images of wolves and trees and a waterfall. She could feel a cool breeze and she closed her eyes and kissed the man. He wrapped his arms around her and passionately kissed her and whispered in her ear. Giselle couldn't make out what the stranger in her dreams was saying but it was soothing and his words made her feel excited. She continued tossing and turning and then began to make low moaning sounds as the man touched her body all over, slowly raking his fingers across her stomach and chest, as he kissed her neck.

Giselle wanted him. She wanted him inside her. But the man continued with his touches which were warm and deliberate, causing her to have an orgasm. Giselle let out a loud moan then jerked awake and looked around. She was panting and tried to catch her breath. She realized that she'd had an orgasm and sat up. She turned on her lamp and looked around. She looked perplexed and was shocked and confused. She got up slowly fearing the worst. That maybe her house guest had been in her room and that maybe, they had sex. *That was just a dream Giselle,* she thought, as she made her way to the stairs.

She stood at the top and looked down over the railing and into the living room. She relaxed when she saw that the man was still laying on her couch. She walked down the steps and over to him then stood over him in the dark. She stared at him. She wondered about him. Giselle was still breathing fast and was still excited from the romantic and erotic sexual dream she'd just had. She stood there desiring a man she didn't know. *I don't even know him. Why am I drawn to him?* she thought as she stood there. *Ok. This is insane. Go back to bed Giselle.*

Giselle walked away and up the stairs, looking back once more. She paused when she got to the top step then went back to her room and closed the door. Alonzo was awake. He hadn't been to sleep. He lay laid there thinking about Giselle all night. He channeled her and made love to her as through her mind and spirit. They were connected. She didn't understand. What was happening her was destiny. Alonzo lay there with his eyes open and still channeling her thoughts and feelings. As she sat in her room, he read her thoughts. He knew she wanted him. He wanted her. For now, he could only have her through their spiritual connection. But he was happy she now desired him. She was desiring him more intensely and he was relishing the moment.

The next morning Giselle woke up and for a second, almost forgot that there was a man asleep on her couch. She awoke as if it had all been some crazy dream. She rose out of bed and walked toward the steps and looked around at her empty house. *Where did he go?* she asked herself, as she walked down the steps and through the house. As she walked through the hall a stern knock startled her. "Who is it?" she yelled, as she made her way to the door. "It's Grant," he replied.

Giselle instantly knew how he ended up on her door at eight in the morning. Ming had to have called him out on concern after no one fitting the description or injuries she described, showed up at the hospital the night before. "Hold on," she replied, as she neared the door. "Grant," she said, as he walked right past her. Giselle rolled her eyes. "Ming told me some man was shot and in your driveway. That you brought him in your home. That you were supposed to call an ambulance for him. What happened Giselle?" he said.

"Grant. I called you several times. Yes, some man was hurt on my road and I helped him out. He's gone now. You couldn't answer your phone, but then show up the next day demanding answers," she criticized. "I was worried Giselle. Where did he go? Ming said he was shot. Was he?" he asked, looking around. "Grant. It's over. He's gone. There's nothing to investigate," she replied. Grant walked over to her window and picked up the bowl that had a small smudge of blood on the side and look inside. "This is a bullet. It looks like a Black Talon slug. Where did you get this?" he asked, looking intently at her. Giselle noticed his mood change and his now more serious tone and was reluctant to tell him anything. But she answered him hoping that he would be satisfied and leave.

"Yes Grant. That was in his back. I grabbed it with a pair of tweezers," she said. "What. That's impossible. This is a Black Talon bullet. Even twenty two caliber bullets won't be sitting on the surface. What do you mean Giselle?" he asked, sounding confused. "I'm know a little about guns. But somehow it was only on the surface. I know what I saw. What is a Black Talon Bullet?" she asked.

"A bullet powerful enough to bring most animals down. Large animals. And you were able to get it out with tweezers? I don't think so. This isn't from a BB gun. Bullets don't sit on the surface of a person's skin. And these were special bullets that no one here has but me. Bullets that would go through a person. Rip their insides. They're lethal. And they're illegal in Idaho," he assured, as he placed the slug in a napkin for safekeeping. "You've been shooting? Shooting around here? Please tell me that you haven't been hunting animals Grant. See... This is what I'm talking about. And you shot that poor man by mistake. What the fuck is wrong with you Grant," she stressed, as she shook her head.

"Giselle I'm sorry I didn't tell you. But you knew I had the kill order. So yes. We went through Wallowa Forest looking for wolves and I shot one. I only shot my gun once. One time." Grant looked puzzled but then had a look of clarity. As if realizing something for the first time. "It's true," he said in a low voice to himself, as Giselle looked at him. "What's true," she asked. "Nothing. I got to go. I'll call you later," he replied. "Wait! What's true Grant?" she asked, as she walked behind him. "Nothing," he repeated. "Don't go shooting again Grant. I mean it," she cautioned. "I have to," he replied, with eyes that looked serious and determined. "I asked you not to shoot the animals. Now you've shot an innocent bystander. You had to have shot more than once. Please stop," she replied.

Grant gave her a quick kiss before she could turn away. "I have to," he said, looking in her eyes. Grant walked to his car then pulled off. Giselle watched from her door. Grant was on some kind of mission that she didn't understand. There was more to it. No animal killings had been reported in some time in Kamiah. She wondered why he was fixated on wolves.

Alonzo stood three hundred feet away perched in a tree watching Giselle and Alonzo. He watched Grant as he drove down her driveway slowly. Giselle looked upset. Her thoughts and feelings reflected a woman who had pulled away from a man. Alonzo could sense her disconnect from Grant. He longed for her and from that distance would be able to smell her if she were to step outdoors. He sat in the same spot that he sat in night after night. The one he was at whenever he wasn't busy with the pack or running around the town working as a landscaper. He watched, trying to read her mind which was a jumbled mix of emotions. He didn't want to channel into her sexually and risk her having sex with Grant out of convenience. He had read her mind enough to know that she was pulling away from Grant.

But he still worried about his presence in her life because he was still a threat. Grant mattered to Giselle. And so that fact meant that she could be vulnerable to Grant and end up back with him at any moment. And that would disrupt their connection and make it more difficult to capture her heart. But equally as important was the fact that Grant was on a mission to kill wolves, namely him. And he needed to bring it to an end. Even if it meant killing Grant.

"Grant, please leave. Stop popping up on me. I had a long, crazy night. I just want to relax. Call me before you come to my house and don't shoot anything on my property. How many times do we have to have this conversation?" she said, disappointed that he had taken on a mission to harm an animal that had saved her life. "Why are you mad at me. This is not my fault Giselle. I have a job to do. Livestock is a way of life for a lot of people. You're being unreasonable. That wolf may have saved you, but it's still a wild animal and dangerous. It was ready to kill me right outside your door and you could care less," he said. Giselle looked at him and did not respond which upset him. "You care more about a damn wolf than me," he accused, looking at her for some sort of indication she did care.

When Giselle held her stare with no response, he stormed out, slamming her door and sped off. Giselle watched as he drove down her road until his car was out of sight. As she walked away from the window, she became warm and felt a strange and powerful sexual feeling come over her. It was more intense than any of the others and she was unable to move. She leaned up against the wall as her vagina throbbed. Giselle reached down into her pants touched her vagina as she moaned. *What the fuck,* she said, as she closed her eyes and had another uncontrollable orgasm that lasted several minutes and had her immobilized. After a few minutes it went away just as swiftly as it came. Giselle opened her eyes and looked around as if she was embarrassed. She smiled and closed her eyes. She liked her spontaneous orgasms that came out of nowhere. They were more fulfilling that any real sex she'd had. Grant had never made her feel that way. The feeling was indescribable. But there was something else. She felt a presence. As though she was being watched. She walked to the adjacent window that faced the forest and looked out through the trees. She stood there and paused before walking away, smiling and feeling exhilarated.

Grant drove straight to a buddy of his who worked at a medical testing laboratory. "Hey Grant," he said, as he entered the lobby. Grant reached in his pocket and handed the man the napkin. "I tried to be careful and not touch it too much. I need to know what's on it," he said. The technician looked at him curiously. "Am I just doing DNA testing? What do you mean what's on it?" the technician asked. "Can you tell me if it's human or not? I shot a wolf and this turned up in a man," he said. "Oh yeah. That can be done. Give me a while though. I'll get right on it. But I won't have answers in a day. You know what I mean," he said. "Yep. But it is a priority," Grant advised. Grant left and headed back to his office. He was anxious to get the results back. Nothing made sense. He was sure he shot his gun once.

Chapter Six - The Hunt

"Good morning," Giselle greeted the secretary, as she walked into *Dataworks*. She glowed from the after-effects of her exuberant and sexually charged evening. She'd had multiple wet dreams throughout the night that she no longer questioned and welcomed. She looked forward to them. They all but consumed her. She was having daily orgasms and she couldn't be happier. It was more than the orgasms for her. There was an inner warmth and satisfaction that had her feeling complete.

It was the best sex she ever had in her life and it was happening through her dreams. And she had a desire for someone she just met. The man everyone was talking about. The one who ended up on her property and who she couldn't stop thinking about. She'd been thinking of him all morning, non-stop and had plans to go to the coffee shop. She hadn't seen him since that night. She hoped he was well. She was concerned. And she wanted to see him again. She was hoping he would be there. He always was.

"Hi Mr. Garner," Giselle said, beaming as she walked past him. He was used to Giselle being in a good mood but this was more than a good mood and he took notice. Mr. Garner walked up to the secretary and handed her his hand-written itinerary so she could add the information to his calendar. "Is something going on that I don't know about?" he asked. "No. Not that I know of. Why?" Beth asked. "You notice something different about Giselle? She's usually so serious looking. She's usually all business. Am I missing something? She getting married or something?" he asked.

Mr. Garner loved office gossip and being in the middle of what everyone was doing. It was the only source of excitement he ever got. "No. But if I hear something, you'll be the first to know," she said, smiling at him. Beth was also wondering what was up with the office "it" girl. The beautiful one who seemed to have it all. Giselle was envied but well liked and Beth liked to keep up with her. She imagined Giselle having the best life a woman could ask for. Beautiful enough to be pursued by all the available bachelors in town. She was smart, witty and currently dating the hot and sexy town sheriff.

"Knock. Knock," Beth said, standing in Giselle's office doorway. "Oh! Come in Beth. I was just going over something. You have that list of old clients I asked for?" she said. "Yes. I have everything right here. I was unable to open up files on any client prior to 1990. That's when we changed systems and we lost a lot of data. But there are over 200 companies listed here. Some here, others in Craigmont and a few in the surrounding towns." Giselle took the list and glanced over it then looked up at Beth and smiled. "Thanks," she said. Giselle opened up her laptop and then looked at the clock. It was still early. She didn't think Alonzo would be at the coffee shop yet and so she would need to wait. *Ok. Giselle. Now you're stalking the man*, she thought, as she smiled to herself. She couldn't stop thinking of him and wanted to see him. She had no way of getting in contact with him and all she could do was hope that they bumped into each other again.

Beth walked back to Giselle's office and knocked lightly. "Hey. Come in," she said. She liked Beth. She was one of the nicest and smartest people in the office. Giselle knew she was undervalued, overworked and underpaid and planned on doing something about it. Beth walked up to her desk. "Can I ask you something personal?" Beth shyly asked. "Sure," Giselle replied. "Who does your makeup? You always look so well put together. I met up with a guy I used to date in high school and he asked me out and I'm nervous. I want to impress him, but I could never do makeup. I just want to be pretty when I go out," she said.

Giselle smiled. She didn't have on much makeup and usually only wore lipgloss. "That's sweet Beth. And you are pretty. You don't need makeup. But I can show you some tricks to enhance your features. I just have on a little powder and lipgloss. And mascara of course. I could show you how. You can come to my house Friday and we can do some different looks," she offered. "Oh Giselle. I don't want to be a bother," Beth replied. "No worries. I'll text you my address and you come to my house around five. I'm usually bored and not doing anything. I could use the company," she admitted. "Oh. Ok. Wow. Thanks. I really appreciate it," she said, as she smiled and left out.

Giselle turned on her computer and loaded a new web design template and went to work for one of their newer clients' page. "Beth can you come here for a minute," she spoke through the phone's paging system. "Sure." Giselle looked over the specifications that Beth had entered and submitted into Giselle's file. "Hey," Beth said, as she walked into her office. "I'm working on the web page for the gentleman who owns a landscaping business? Did he say what the basic function of the page was for? I mean. It doesn't say if he needs it set up to respond to emails. I also can't tell whether he wants to sell his services through his page or is it basically like a landing page where it just has facts and great graphics. The specifications don't mention the need for plug-ins either. Does he want the ability to capture client information? Even the name of the

company is missing? He's giving me nothing to
work with," she noted.

"I'm sorry Giselle. He called in. He was
short and quick. But he's paid in full even though I
told him he only needed to start with a deposit. I told
him that he needed to review and approve a basic
layout at which point he could then pay us in full. He
asked for you specifically. I have his address and
phone number. I can try calling him," she said.
Giselle looked off. "He asked for me. A referral
perhaps," she asked. DataWorks did not typically
work by referrals. Clients were set up with which
ever wed designer was available to do the work. It
depended on availability and what the client's needs
were. Giselle and a gentleman named Andy, that
they affectionately called CyberMaster, were
assigned the more complicated clients. *How would
he know to ask for me?* she thought. "Yeah. Can you
get him on the phone and send him to me?" she
asked. "Ok. I'll call him now."

Alonzo was working at a new client's home when he looked at his phone. He smiled and put the phone back in his pocket. He continued to cut and carry the wood he would be using for Mrs. Howards backyard as she watched from her window. Mrs. Howard stared at the handsome and robust looking gentleman she had just hired while her husband was away on a business trip. She'd lusted over him since observing him in the yard of her neighbor and close friend Amelia Stanton's yard. She was completely enthralled with him and saw what Amelia meant by he was *great* to watch. Alonzo knew she was watching. He was used to being watched. He understood his appeal and attraction to the opposite sex. But his affections were for one woman. He wanted and desired only one woman. He had plans to love only one woman for the rest of his life. And her name was Giselle Marie Jackson.

"Ok. Mrs Howard. So, I started your garden but I need you to look at it. See if you like the design so far, before I continue," Alonzo said. He was mesmerizing when he talked and Mrs. Howard hadn't heard a word he said. "Huh," she said, embarrassed that she hadn't paid attention to the words that came out of his mouth. She was too busy fantasizing about him. She was hoping he would give her a sign. Any indication that he was interested in a romp in the sack with her. "Can you take a look at what I've done so far," he repeated. Mrs. Howard exited her home, smiling and making small talk as she walked back towards her garden.

"It's lovely Alonzo. Stunning. When will you be back to finish it?" she asked, as she gazed into his eyes. Mrs. Howard was a week away from her 61st birthday and the only birthday gift she wanted was a night with Alonzo. Her and Mr. Howard hadn't been intimate in some time. But managed to maintain a close bond despite the lack of sex in their marriage. "I'll be back to finish up tomorrow if that works for you," he replied.

Alonzo looked at his phone again and saw his caller id showed another call from *DataWorks*. He wasn't prepared to speak with Giselle and so he let the call go to his voicemail. But the idea of her contacting him made him blush. He was excited. It was something he waited a long time for. Years in fact. Alonzo felt overwhelmed. He wanted to take his time. She was important. She was his lifeline. A fact that may overwhelm her and run her off, if she knew. He didn't think she would believe him. And he wasn't sure she was strong enough to deal with such complications. Humans were weaker than wolves. They required a certain amount of assurances. A certain amount of normalcy. Words that just weren't part of his vocabulary. His life was anything but. "Ok. So, I'll see you first thing in the morning," Alonzo said to Mrs. Howard as he walked to his suburban.

"Giselle. I had to leave a message. No one is picking up," Beth stated. "But I can't start unless I have more information. Keep trying him. What's the address he gave? Did you look it up? Is it a residence or a business location?" Giselle* asked. "It's a home address. I believe he runs the business from home," Beth replied. "What's the address?" Giselle asked. "3120 Valley Road in Kamiah," Beth replied. *Wow. That's near me. Like a few miles up the road,* she thought. "Ok. Thanks. Keep trying him."

Giselle shut down the project and began working on another client's website. She stopped working and stared out into the lobby. Grant had entered and was standing at the receptionist station talking to Beth. Giselle sighed then shook her head. He was the last person she wanted to see. "Giselle. You have a guest," Beth stated. "Ok. Send him back," she replied. Grant walked through as the women in the office watched. Everyone knew who Sheriff Ellis was. He was the hot and sexy sheriff who took himself way too seriously and was head over heels in love with one of their executives.

"Hey Giselle," he said, walking into her office and sitting at her desk. "What is it Grant," she said, looking up at him blank faced then back at her computer. "You're still mad. Come on Giselle. I miss you. This is crazy. Why is everything, both man and animal, getting treated better than I am," he asked looking as though he hadn't slept in days. "You still out shooting animals," she asked, then looked at him. Grant looked over his shoulder then back at her and didn't answer. Giselle rolled her eyes and continued her work while he sat there. He tried to think of something to say that would get her to see his side of things.

"I love you Giselle. I'm not going away just because you're mad. I'll call you later," he said, as he rose from the chair. He walked around her desk and kissed her on the cheek. Giselle continued typing and watched as he left out. She was angry beyond comprehension and done with any remnants of a relationship with him.

Grant drove toward his office and radioed his secretary Marguerite. She was supposed to assemble a hunt team to go deeper into Wallowa Forest. But only fourteen men showed up. Grant wanted a team of twenty men due to the size of the pack. Their numbers were rumored to be around 12- 15 and so Grant wanted no less than twenty men. "Marguerite. Did more people show up?" he asked. "No. Not really. You still have about the same. But one of the men here said you should go and talk to Chitto Kituah's family. They say that this mission is a death sentence. Can you go speak to the family first," she pleaded. "I will if it will make everyone feel better. But I hope you know I don't believe in superstition," he replied.

Grant pulled down an old dirt trail that went for half a mile before pulling in front of the Kituah family home. It was a large, one story wood home, painted three different colors with scrap metal for a roof. As soon as Grant pulled in the father and matriarch of all the living Kituah members came out and stood on the porch. He was as wise as he looked, with his long grey silky hair and smooth but wrinkled skin. Chitto had a reputation in town for sensing things like bad weather and earthquakes before they occurred.

"Hey Chitto. I was told to speak to you before my team heads out. That you had information that may be of use," he said, squinting from the sun. "I have nothing useful. I have a warning. What you are seeking you will not find. What you hunt and seek to kill, knows you are coming and the spirits of the forest have spoken against you. Your mission will fail and men will die. The wolf you seek is not a wolf. There are two of them and they are each other's enemy. And if you kill the wrong one, you will see more death and more killing of the livestock. One keeps the other in check. It is the one whose spirit is unclean that has been doing all the killing of the livestock. If you do not murder him and shoot the one that had been protecting us, we will pay tenfold," he warned.

Grant looked around. Chitto's words sounded like inflated wives tales and nothing more. "What do you mean by the wolves are not wolves?" he asked. Chitto stared at him and took a long pause before answering. He could sense that Grant did not believe him and so he was ready to end the conversation. Chitto hated to get involved. He didn't like when men set out to kill animals. He believed that animals were spirits that enlightened and engaged with the world as we all did and deserved respect. "The wolf is a spirit. Not a wolf. He is like us," he replied.

Grant extended his hand and Chitto shook it then looked at him with a different face. Grant noticed the change in him then turned slowly and headed back to his car. He looked back at Chitto. His words made an impact. Grant grew concerned. The Kituah family was highly respected and Chitto was a visionary. They called him the oracle. He was considered the most enlightened prophet. Grant got in his car and started the engine, and waved but Chitto didn't wave back. Before Grant pulled off a woman came out and walked down off the porch and stood next to Chitto. "Are they still going to kill the wolves," she said. Chitto paused. "Yes. I was not successful in deterring him. But... this man is not doing it for the sake of livestock, he's doing it over a woman."

Alonzo drove up the road and slammed on his breaks and stared off into the trees. He could sense trouble for his pack and parked on the side of the desolate road. He looked around to see if anyone was near, then began running and jumped in the air. He changed into Blackwolf before his feet hit the ground. He ran full speed through the vegetation for miles. He could smell the scent of death in the air. He could feel his packs sadness. He ran until he reached the howling pack, mourning the loss of another strong and powerful beta wolf.

Blackwolf walked in between the members and up to the dead wolf torn to shreds. It was an obvious attack by another wolf. It was one of their oldest and dearest members whose instincts and hunting ability were unmatched. He was the one Blackwolf relied upon whenever he needed to be away. Blackwolf depended on the beta to keep the pack fed and strong. He was away a lot and was trying to prepare the pack for the day he would no longer be there. He wanted to live his life mostly in human form and was taking longer stays away from them. He needed to be in human form more often. If he was ever going to win the heart of the woman he loved.

This was a tremendous loss for the pack. The beta had fearless fighting abilities and was dedicated to the pack. The wolf probably loss its life standing up to Darius and his pack. Blackwolf looked around and saw two more injured but alive wolves. Darius was killing his pack family slowly and methodically. One by one. And Blackwolf could not stay in wolf form in order to protect them. He had a more pressing matter at hand. He had just one year and two months or 14.2 moons before he would have to remain a wolf forever. He needed to be in man form more than wolf form. It was the only way to ensure that Giselle had all the time she needed to fall in love with him and break the curse.

He could not rush it and he could not speak it or the curse would not be lifted. She had to fall in love with him naturally. And he would have to consummate their union in order for it to work. But losing this beta was a major blow to his plans. Without him, he would have to split his time and be with the pack even more. Darius would kill them one by one quicker, now that the strongest ones were dead. Blackwolf howled as loud as he could which lead to the howling of the others wolves. Grant got out of his car and looked to the forest. He could hear them. *We're coming. Just sit tight. Your days are numbered,* he said, as he walked into his office.

Grant and his men drove on the rocky terrain in their Jeep 4x4's and Ford Pickups hauling their ATV's and carrying high powered rifles for another day of wolf hunting. They had been unsuccessful and Grant was becoming desperate. As the men made their hike through some of the rougher areas, they looked around watching for any signs of the pack. Grant was as serious and as determined as ever. He didn't speak a single word to anyone as he sat next to the driver of the car he rode in.

The driver looked over at Grant and looked back to the road. He had been on many hunt missions with Grant over the years. Some involved mountain lions and bears but he couldn't recall going so deep in to get the animals. This was like a manhunt. The deeper in the more dangerous and the men were feeling vulnerable. There were snakes, wild boar and other dangerous animals plus the small chance that they could lose their bearings and get lost. Grant was skilled at hiking and survival in harsh environments. He had knowledge of wolves and their patterns. Information he had learned as a child growing up and would later use as an adult.

Grant remained quiet as the driver of their Jeep slowed. All the cars pulled over near Snake River and parked to continue on, using their three and four wheeler ATV's. "Ok. So listen up. We're going to do three teams of five men. We're heading north but we need to be at least two hundred feet from one another to cover more ground. Use the radio and start a contained smoke fire if you get lost.

Any questions," he asked. The men were armed and ready and after Grants instruction, headed north hoping to run into the pack.

Chapter Seven - The Other Hunt

Giselle looked at her watch. It was noon and she became anxious. It was the same time she had seen Alonzo at the coffee shop before. And so she decided to stop what she was doing and go there for a Cappuccino and a snack. She got up from her desk and went to the bathroom to check her makeup. She grabbed her purse and then walked towards the front of the office and up to Beth's desk. "I'm running to *The Beanery* coffee shop. You want something?" she asked. "No. I'm ok. I can go for you if your busy?" she asked. "No. I need a break and I want to take a walk. I won't be long," she said, as she left.

Giselle was nervous. She was excited. She felt a bevy of emotions like a school girl going to meet a guy for the first time. She hoped he'd be there. The closer she got to the coffee shop the more nervous she became. *What will I say to him? Oh no. What if he's married? I didn't think about that,* she thought, as she got closer to the shop. Giselle looked through their wide picture window as she walked to the door and was disappointed that she didn't see him. *Ok. I'll order something and just wait a minute. But I can't stay. I have to finish my work.*

The shop was quiet and serene. Giselle drank her coffee slowly and looked around. It wasn't as busy as it could get when noon time arrived. Giselle sat back and got comfortable, hoping she wouldn't have to wait long. She pulled out her phone and played Bejeweled as she waited. Over an hour had gone by and there was no sign of him. *It figures,* she thought, as she shut the Bejeweled app down and walked towards the door. She paused for a minute then turned around and walked to the counter.

"Hi. Um. Can I talk to you for a minute?" she said. The young lady, whose face Giselle recognized as one of the women who flirted with Alonzo, looked puzzled but agreed to speak with her.

The two went outside and Giselle got right to the point. "Um. I wanted to ask you. You know that handsome dark skinned, nice built man that comes in here sometimes," she asked pausing as she could see the girls face light up. It was obvious the woman knew exactly who she was talking about. "Yes," she replied. Giselle smiled and continued. "Yeah. Him. Well, I wanted to ask. Have you seen him lately? I need to talk to him." The woman looked at her and smiled. "No. He only comes here when you're in here. Seriously. We thought you two were secret lovers. I'm kinda surprised you're asking me about him. I thought you knew him. Like really knew him. We envy you. It's obvious he has some sort of feelings for you," the woman replied.

Giselle smiled and looked away. The other barista had already told her this but she was wondering if anything had changed. She couldn't help but wonder why he was only coming in when she was there? How would he know when those times would be and why wasn't he there now. "You ever bump into him anywhere else?" Giselle asked. "Well. One time I saw him near my uncles' home. He was walking into the woods. I was wondering what he was doing and he just walked and never looked back. Straight into the forest and never stopped. Like he was going somewhere. No gun to hunt. No fishing gear to catch fish. Nothing. I thought that was strange. He walked with purpose. Like he had a specific place to be," she said. Giselle looked off into the mountains. "Thanks. Do me a favor if he ever comes here will you call me," she said, handing the woman her business card. "Sure. But he won't come unless you're here."

Giselle walked back into her office and Beth immediately noticed her change in demeanor. "Everything ok," she asked. "Oh. Yeah. I'm ok," she replied. Giselle went to her office and closed her door and sat at her desk unable to concentrate. She doodled on her desk notepad and looked out the window. *Get a grip. You don't even know him. Why are you so concerned?* Giselle opened up her web program and opened the template. She tried to work on the newly created web page but was unable to stay focused. She closed down the template and began working on a written proposal she had started. But again, was unable to focus and closed out of her PowerPoint. Giselle sighed. She began to question her desire to see the man she barely knew. *You don't know him,* she thought and shook her head in disbelief. She shut her laptop in frustration and got up and walked to her window. She stood there staring at the very spot he would stand at. *Where are you?*

Grant and his men were growing tired and exhausted from the heat and were almost ready to give up. But grant pushed the men, continually reminding them of the livestock that either they or their neighbor had lost. A tactic that worked. The men would have a new-found zest to finish what they came to do. They circled back and went northwest searching high and low for the pack. Just as Grant was ready to try again another day, one of the men radioed that he saw something in the distance. Grant found renewed energy and grabbed the walkie talkie. "Where. What do you see?" he said, waiting eagerly for a response. "Something's running through the grassy area over here. We're going in," he said. "No! Wait for us. Hello! Hello!" Grant repeated and got no answer. "Damn. He never said where."

Grant looked around and then signaled for the men within view to drive over to him. Three men on ATV's came to him. "Ok. So, you heard what he said. And now we've lost contact with him. But he said he saw something. Anyone recognize the voice? Who was that?" he asked. One of the men blurted "It sounded like Steve Mitchell but I can't say for certain."

Grant looked around and saw another man on a ATV and waved him over. "Ok. We'll look for him and do not chase after anything. Use your scope and try to get the best shot you can." Grant waited for the other man on the ATV to get to them and watched as he neared. "Hey what's up. I dropped my walkie talkie somewhere while I was riding," the man said. "Don't worry about that. Listen. We lost contact with someone. Perez seems to think it may be Steve. We need to go find him and make sure he's ok. The last time we talked to him he was saying he saw something in the grass. Since you no longer have your radio, I'm going to need you to stay close to me. We're not risking men," Grant stated.

"Ok. Let's go. Let's head north. Spread out but do not go out of view of whoever your riding next to." The men pulled off and drove up the hill headed further northwest. After several minutes of searching one of the drivers came upon the abandoned ATV with blood covering it and even more on the ground. The driver looked around. The hunter was nowhere in sight. He sighed and dropped his head then radioed for help. "Hey. I got something over here where the trees get more dense. I was on the outskirt so, should be to your left," he said, as he grabbed his weapon and got off his ATV. Grant pointed and the men close to him turned left and headed to a group of trees close together. Grant looked around and saw that the other men heard the transmission and were also headed to the area.

Grant was trailing behind them and saw the men with their heads down standing near one of the four wheelers. He pulled up and jumped off and walked past the men as they just stared at him. "Where is he?" he asked. "He's not here. Whatever did this, took him," one of the men said. Grant took his hat off and kneeled down. "This is a lot of blood. Steve is a big guy. What could carry him off. He has to be, what? Three hundred pounds or so," Grant said, looking confused and worried. The men shook their heads yes. "Look. I know a little something about behaviors and animals and what their capable of. No wolf would be able to drag a three hundred pound man and it wouldn't even try. They eat where they kill. Same as a bear. Unless the prey is small and easy for them to grab and take away. What is this, cause it ain't no wolf," one of the men said.

The other men all looked at Grant. "I don't know ok. Just let me think," Grant replied, looking around. One of the other hunters chimed in. "Look Grant. I thought this would be an easy assignment. Shoot wolves that are killing livestock. No problem. But one of us just got killed. I'm not going any further. I cannot risk my life for this. I have kids," the man said. The other men all shook their heads in agreement as they were thinking the same thing. No one wanted to disappoint Grant, but they had families to consider. They had all heard about the rumors of the forest. And now they were seeing it first-hand.

The rumor centered around a story about the wolves being spirits and that trying to kill a wolf would result in loss of life. And the fact that Kamiah had hunters that were killed by wolves in the past, had the men spooked. The hunters were always found torn to pieces, with no witnesses. "We can't just give up. If we stick together and not span out alone, we can prevent this from happening again," Grant stated. "And what about the rumors that these wolves are difficult to kill and larger than normal. What if there is a curse? Some say these wolves are spirits not real wolves. I second Rob. We should just go. We need, like, the army or something. More men. More powerful weapons and better protection. We're vulnerable."

Grant could see that the men were afraid and had lost their drive. He worried that if he pushed them, they would make mistakes that could cost them their lives. "Ok. But we have to at least try and find Steve's body first." The men got on their ATV's and searched the area for nearly two hours then called off the search as dusk approached. They headed back south towards their vehicles and left the forest.

The men went back into town and went their separate ways as Grant drove back to the station. Grant got out and slammed his car door in frustration as his deputies looked on. The three men walked into the station, solemn and quiet. Grant greeted Marguerite then went into his office and closed the door. "Geez. What's his problem?" she asked the deputies. "We didn't get anything and we loss Steve Mitchell. Marguerite gasped. "What! How?" she asked, as she teared up. She knew Steve Mitchell. His family was active in the community and he was a likeable guy with a wife and kids. The deputy paused and looked down. "Not sure. Something killed him. There was tons of blood. We tried to locate his body but we couldn't find him," he said.

The deputies sat at their desk and took a couple of calls about reckless driving and vandalism. They wrote the reports and waited on Grant to exit his office. An hour went by as other deputies returned to the station from working the streets. They were all aware of what had happened. Word travelled fast in their small town and they knew it was only a matter of time before Steve's wife Melissa would be there.

Grant finally emerged from his office more upset than when he walked in. "I can't get any help. Even after someone has died, the government won't send anyone to help. Said we can't use government resources for a wolf problem. Then hung up on me when I told them these were large wolves and that they were hard to kill. Laughed at me. Like I was joking," he said, fuming. Grant stood there for a minute then stormed out and walked past everyone without saying anything and left. He got in his car and pulled off as his deputies walked out to check on him.

Grant drove home. He needed a break from everything. He was frustrated and wanted answers. "This is unreal. I know this is all tied together. The strange man seen around town. And the strange things that keep happening around Giselle. It's just like my grandfather warned me about. This shit is happening just like he said it would." Grant said, as he continued towards his home, talking to himself about what his grandfather had experienced and had talked to him about.

History seemed to be repeating itself. Grants grandfather told him about a man that had come to town. Not long after his arrival, strange things began to happen. He told Grant that as soon as the man had arrived, wolf activity in their area increased and animals were being ripped apart in unnatural ways. Even for a predator. That some of the animals killed were killed for sport and weren't consumed. He told him that the man seemed obsessed with a local woman and that she eventually became obsessed with him. He told him that the two of them eventually went away and he never saw the man again. He told Grant that the woman's family never heard from her again and that after they left, wolf activity returned to normal. That no livestock were killed. The only dead animals were the predators' natural prey which were forest animals such as small critters and larger animals like the deer and Elk.

Grant worried because he still hadn't seen the new resident that people had described. It was almost as if the man was purposely avoiding him. Like he knew where Grant would be and was avoiding those places. Kamiah was a small town and it wasn't easy to avoid being seen for such a long period of time. Grant was now determined that he needed to locate the new resident. He would put his wolf hunt on hold and find the elusive man and see if there was a connection. And Grant believed, that in order to find him, he would need to stay close to Giselle.

Giselle ran bath water after her long day at work. She walked through her home in a short silk and lace gown, lighting candles throughout to help relax her. She walked into her front room and turned on her cd player. Then walked into the kitchen and poured herself a glass of water. She smiled when Marvin Gaye's *What's Going On* played. She had her speakers situated throughout her house. She sat her glass down and started swaying to the music and closed her eyes as it resonated with her soul.

Giselle danced slowly as she walked towards the stairs then jogged up the stairs and walked down the hall and into her bedroom. Giselle loved the freedom of being the only home in her immediate area. And she wasn't shy about walking around nude which she did frequently despite objections from Grant at the time. There were no neighbors near that could see her. No one watching. Or so she thought. She was not aware that she was being watched. From a tree. At that moment.

Alonzo sat, in the dark, on the thick wide branch and watched as Giselle danced and closed her eyes. She moved in a sensual and sexy way which turned him on. He could hear her music as she thought about the lyrics. As she tuned in to each strike of the drum and the keys of the piano. He stared at her and couldn't help but get turned on. And the more turned on he became, the more he channeled her which cause her to feel aroused herself.

Giselle touched her body and then opened her eyes as she felt more aroused. She walked over to her dresser and grabbed her sex toys and climbed into her bed. She was too aroused to ignore and decided she would make herself come but it was too late. Alonzo was already doing that and before she could even touch her vagina, she screamed out in ecstasy as she had a powerful orgasm. She grabbed her sheets and grabbed her vagina, disregarding the dildo in her hand. Alonzo watched as she rubbed her self softly at first then more vigorously moaning and moving her body as if she was having sex.

Giselle had tuned completely out and was on her third orgasm when she opened her eyes and stopped and looked out her window. She sat up and cut her lamp off and look in the darkness as she panted. She looked on the ground then in the trees and thought she saw a man. *Somethings happening to me. This is no coincidence,* she said, as she stared at the tree and tried to focus but the distance was just too great. When she looked back down at the ground, she saw a man walking away from the tree and into the dense vegetation.

Giselle grabbed her gown and then put her robe over top and slipped on her house shoes. She ran out her sliding door and down the back stairway her father built. It was a beautifully done treated-wood staircase with etched pictures of animals in the wood. "Wait," she yelled, as she ran toward the woods. Giselle tried to run fast but the house shoes she had on, were terrible for running. She could only go so fast without falling. She slowed down and walked into the forest looking around for what she thought was Alonzo. It was something about the man's body and the way he walked. She would recognize that walk anywhere.

But going into a forest at night was asking for trouble. An animal would attack at night, especially if it hadn't eaten. Giselle walked a few feet in and stopped. She sighed as she looked around. She had looked for him every day and wanted to find him. She was drawn to him and she wanted to know him. Alonzo watched her from behind a huge tree just a few feet away from her. Giselle closed her eyes and then looked toward the tree he was standing at but Alonzo was no longer visible and so she stared at the tree for a minute but then looked around, scanning the area for any sight of the man.

She sighed again and then turned and walked back toward her home as Alonzo watched her. He wasn't sure how she would handle knowing he watched her from trees. He wasn't sure how she would handle anything about his different and complicated life. But he wanted his life with her as normal as possible. He knew she would need that. A normal life. A regular life like everyone else. He wasn't sure she could handle much more than that. And if it wasn't for the fact that he had to spend a lot more time in the forest, he would have made his introduction. He would have tried to be a part of her life. But with both Darius and Grant hunting his pack, the timing was bad. He needed just a short time. He planned on annihilating his enemies swiftly. He needed a plan. To go at them impulsively, could cost him.

He could tell that she was channeled into him. She should not have been able to sense that he was in the trees. That fact made him happy. It meant that she was falling for him. That she was tuned into him. But he needed to be careful. He had been with her sexually, on a mental level, and he wasn't sure if she would view that as a violation. Would she accept it as something that kindred spirits did and welcome it? She seemed to enjoy it, but he wasn't sure of how she would react knowing those powerful orgasms were his doing.

Giselle walked through her sliding door, closed it and sat on her bed. She took a deep breath and looked over at her phone when it lit up. She saw that Grant was calling her. "Hello," she answered. "Hey. It's me. Can I come see you?" he asked. Alonzo had started to walk away but felt her vibe and then tuned into her thoughts and knew Grant was either on the phone or in her house. He ran back towards her home, emerging from the forest and ran to the back of her house. He walked up the side of the house and looked and didn't see Grants car. He stood there up against her house as she spoke with Grant.

"No Grant. I was just about to get in the tub then go to bed. Plus, I just don't want to see you. I don't like who you've become. I don't look at you the same," she said. "Why is that? Because I'm a man. A man who's trying to protect people. This isn't about me Giselle. You're in love with that guy," he said. Giselle held the phone. She thought for a minute. She was confused. She wanted Alonzo on a level like that of a woman in love. But it was too early for those feelings. She hadn't even kissed the man. The only exchanges that had occurred with Alonzo was a crazy night when he was hurt and she helped him out. Other than finding him sexy and desiring him, she didn't think she loved him. She lusted for him and that wasn't the same thing. "Grant. I don't even know him. But anyway. What is it to you? At least he's not out there killing animals for no reason," she said.

"No. He's killing men and animals," he replied. "What! You will say anything. You're just jealous. Don't call my phone anymore. I never want to hear from you ever," she said, as she hung up. Giselle got up off her bed and walked back to her window. She looked at the trees again, unable to remember which one the man was perched in. She looked on the ground and all around. "I wish you'd come back," she said, as she turned and walked into her bathroom and shut the door. Alonzo heard what she said. He felt compelled to go to her room, knock on her sliding door and enter. He wanted to tell her how he felt then kiss her on her lips. He waited then when he felt the water touch her body, he ran to the forest and disappeared into the night.

Giselle woke up bright and early the next morning and immediately went to the window. She repeatedly went to the window and was disappointed that he wasn't there. It was Friday and she had the whole weekend to herself to relax and make some runs. And if she was lucky, bump into Alonzo. She also remembered that she had promised Beth she would help her do her makeup for the date night she had with her new love interest.

Giselle got ready and put a pot of tea on as she prepared to leave. She drove as she multi tasked, calling her office and taking calls from her friend Ming while she sent calls from Grant to voice mail. *Damn,* she said, as she spilled some of her tea onto her skirt. She was glad her skirt was black and wouldn't show the stain. Giselle's plan was to stop at the address she had from Beth for the new client and get what she needed. She had been unable to begin his website due to the lack of information she had.

"Dammit. What did I do with that information," she said, as she searched through a pile of paper. Giselle looked for the paper she wrote the address on as she neared the street. "Ok. It's probably the only house on the road. There's only one house on that road. I think," she thought, as she turned on Valley Road. Giselle pulled up to the impressive, large home. *Wow. I don't remember this home looking like this. The owner must have torn down the other home and built this.* She had been at that location before as a young girl with her father and the home back then was much smaller. She was more than impressed if he did the additions to the house himself. It was the most fabulous log home she'd ever seen with massive think logs stacked precisely and beautiful tall glass windows perfectly clean as if polished daily. The home had a classy yet rustic feel and looked like it cost quite a penny to produce. With its custom symbolic drawings and attention to detail, it was the ultimate in curb appeal.

It was nestled beyond the view of the road just a few feet from the forest. Giselle walked to the home looking around. It had a deserted look as if the owners were away on vacation. She walked up to the door and knocked then eased to the window and peeked in. Alonzo was in the forest when his senses picked up Giselle's anxiety. He focused on her thoughts and then realized she was at his house. He ran through the forest, topping his own speed as he zoomed through the forest at speeds close to 110 mph. Giselle looked in the window and then reached in her briefcase and pulled out one of her business cards and walked back to her car. She pulled off and called Beth. "Beth. Are you sure about the address? The house looked deserted," she said, as she drove away then glanced in her rear-view mirror.

Giselle slammed on her brakes and looked back. She was in shock. It was Alonzo. Standing in the driveway and watching as she drove away. "Um. Let me call you back," she said, as she smiled and hung up then checked herself in the mirror. "Ok Giselle. Get a grip. It's just a man. A fine one but still, just a regular guy. You got this." Giselle backed her car up then turned around and drove back slowly.

Oh my fucking...Is he actually more handsome. What the hell..." she said, as she drove up to him. "Hey," she said, as she rolled her window down. "Hey," he replied smiling and making her heart strings sing.

"Um. Did you need a website? My secretary gave me your address but not much more than that. I was coming by because I haven't been able to start it without more information," she said. Giselle and Alonzo stared at each other for a moment. "You want to come in," he said in the sexiest voice. It was like music to her ears. His look, his smell and his voice made it impossible to turn the offer down. His demeanor calmed her. She didn't second guess anything as he had a way of making her feel safe. It was like she was supposed to be there. She wondered why his presence was so soothing to her. "Um. Ok," she said, as she pulled up a little more then cut her car off.

Giselle got out and Alonzo looked her up and down and smiled which made her blush. Her skirt was a bit too short for work, but Giselle liked pushing the envelope. She dressed however she felt and Alonzo giving her orgasms almost on a daily basis, had her wearing her skirts a little shorter. Alonzo followed her and watched as she walked to his door. Giselle knew he was looking at her and blushed as she walked up the steps and to his open door. Alonzo opened the screen door and Giselle walked in. She looked around at his beautifully decorated home that she had already admired from the window. "You want to sit here," he said. "Yeah. Ok," she replied, sitting down at his dining room table. It was made of heavy duty marble and lacquered wood with the most stunning chairs.

"It's beautiful in here. I'm surprised," she said. "Why," he replied. "Because it's not the typical man cave. Unless your wife helped decorate it. Then I understand," she said, as she looked intensely at him. "No. I live alone and I decorated it myself. I made most of the furniture by hand," he replied. "What!" she said, as she looked around. "Did you make these chairs?" she asked. "Yes," he replied. "Oh. Ok. Um. Well. Let me see what I need," she said, as she nervously pulled his file out of her briefcase and looked through the papers. Alonzo stared at her and looked down at her chest and could see her breaths had increased. He could hear her thoughts and blushed as she fumbled with her papers while her mind drifted. He could hear her thoughts of how good he smelled and how she would love to get naked in front of him at that very moment.

"Ok. So… what I need is the name of the website and what the website will be used for. Is it to tell a story. Or do you want the visitors to your page to be able to book appointments with you. Or… is it for appointments and items you'll be selling and if so, I'll need a list of those items," she said, as she grabbed her eye glasses and put them on. "You look beautiful in those," he said. Giselle smiled and was speechless as she looked at him then turned her attention back to her file.

She felt herself losing control. She was desiring him in a way that she thought was obvious and her anxiety took hold. "It's for booking appointments and showing examples of my work. I have pictures I can email to you," he said. Giselle smiled and shook her head yes. "Yep. Ok. I think that's it for now. I have an appointment so I have to get back. I'll call you if I need anything else. Is the number I have a house or cell number? It always goes to voicemail," she asked. "That's my cell," he replied. "Oh," she said. Alonzo gazed into her eyes and she looked away. "Thanks," she said, as she walked toward the door, opening it and walking out onto the porch.

Alonzo followed her out. "You ok," he asked. "Yeah. Thanks. So, I'll call," she said, as she got in her car and pulled off. Giselle watched him as she drove almost going into the grass. She continued driving down his path towards the main road looking back as he stood watching her. *Two more minutes and I would have been all over him. What is my problem.*

Chapter Eight - Wow Factor

Giselle walked into her office and saw Beth standing in her office doorway talking to someone. "Hey," she spoke, as she walked into her office and right into Grant. "Grant," she said, as she walked past him and to her desk. "Uh. Do you need anything Giselle? I'm going to go back to my desk. Sheriff Ellis just wanted to meet with you," she said, looking at him then back at Giselle. "No Beth. I'm ok. Can you shut my door please?" she replied, as she walked to her window. Beth sensed she was displeased at Grants unannounced visit.

As soon as Beth closed the door, Giselle turned and faced him. "You just don't get it do you. I'm not sure how much more blunt I can be. You ignore every request. Every single one. I've asked that you call me first and not pop up on me and you totally ignore me. I've asked that you not hunt the animal near me and yet you ignored that. That black wolf that saved my life, I haven't seen in weeks. I'm afraid to ask. I know you don't like him because you thought he was going to attack you. But I must ask. Did you kill it? I fed him so the animal would have returned by now. I fed it steak! And I haven't seen it. I know you killed it and I'll never forgive you for that. Never."

Grant walked up to her. "I didn't kill any wolves. Not one. But I am. Just because you're in love with one and can't see straight means nothing to me. You don't know what's going on. You're under his spell," he replied. "What! You sound ridiculous Grant. First off, I'm not in love with a wolf. I just don't want you to bring it harm and secondly, no one has me under a spell," she said. "Really," he replied, looking intently at her. "The new man in town. Don't you find it strange that he appeared out of nowhere and all this shit is happening now. You don't find that odd at all?" he asked, shaking his head in disbelief. "I feel sorry for you. And if all this is for my affections, you are sadly mistaken. I wouldn't dare see you after all you've done. You took men deep in the forest and one died because of your obsession. You need help. Please leave. And don't come back," she stated. Grant turned and stormed away. He believed Giselle was not in her right mind.

Darius trotted gaining momentum as he led his pack deeper into the forest following the scent of Alonzo's pack family. He had followed Alonzo home and knew he was away from the forest. He wanted to seize the moment while his cousin and arch rival was away. He was able to annihilate three members of the pack and either Grant and his men or someone else had killed a fourth. There were only three more beta's a few omega's and one alpha female left. This mission was to kill the alpha female so no new pups would be born into the pack.

Darius picked up his pace as he identified their location. He was determined to destroy the female and whatever male wolf stood in their way. Darius hated his wolf form. The curse that he was unable to remove. He hated that Alonzo seemed close to removing his. He had watched as Alonzo seduced Giselle. He could see she was marked by a wolf and knew that wolf had to be Alonzo. There were no other werewolves except him and Alonzo. Darius never had offspring with a human when he was in human form and so his legacy would die with him. But Alonzo still had time.

The only offspring Darius fathered were wolves with an alpha female and there was no curse on them They were real wolves, with no ability to shift and would live the lifespan of a normal wolf, not up to 300 years as he would. Alonzo was now 29 years old. He had less than a year to break his curse. Darius was thirty two and doomed to live as a wolf unless killed by a silver bullet through the heart or at the jaws or another werewolf.

Alonzo sat on his couch exhausted but fulfilled. He thought of the visit he received from Giselle. How beautiful she was. Her thoughts of attraction towards him melted his heart. He was ready to be with her. But he had a lingering problem. His family of wolves were in trouble. He couldn't just round them up and take them to unknown territory. They knew nothing of his man form. They would try to attack and kill him if he showed himself. They looked at him as 100% wolf. The same as they were. He wasn't sure how they would react to seeing he was a man. Trying to show them he shifted into their leader at will, would probably not be accepted. It could cause confusion and could eventually interfere with the harmony of the pack. And if he tried to show them his human form and they attacked, he would have to kill them. Alonzo knew he would never be the same if he killed his own pack family.

He sat, rubbing his head, trying to think of a solution. He sensed trouble and paused. He stood up and stared as he focused keenly on his senses picking up the smell of fear in the air. The danger was coming from his own pack family as he picked up their scents. Alonzo ran out the door and towards the trees jumping into the air and changing into a wolf and running nearly 100 mph as he jumped wood logs and dodge shrubs headed north through the forest.

He picked up speed and was running 110 mph speeding fast toward Snake River. He jumped over the narrow yet deep river and continued on the path as he closed in on Darius and his pack. Some of the pack saw him coming and took off running. Darius turned around and Blackwolf attacked him from behind, ripping into his shoulder and releasing him and then attacked him ripping into his other shoulder and arm. He growled as he savagely ripped through Darius' flesh.

A few more wolves from Darius' pack ran but two stayed on and one charged Blackwolf from behind. But the wolf was no match for him. Blackwolf turned around and grabbed the wolf, ripping into his throat and pulling out his flesh killing him instantly. Blackwolf walked around Darius in a circle. This was his only cousin. The only real blood family he had and he didn't want to kill him unless he had to. Darius would not back down and although he was strong, he was not stronger than Blackwolf and never prevailed in their battles.

Darius looked into Blackwolf's eyes. He was filled with anger and rage, but then turned around and ran. Blackwolf looked at the last wolf from Darius' pack. A large beta that was crouched in an attack position. He approached the wolf then charged it and took a chunk from its shoulder before it whined and ran away.

Blackwolf walked cautiously through the shrubs, into a clearing and into a slaughterhouse. All the wolves had been killed. Even some of the young ones. He looked at their perfect bodies with no damage and got closer as it wasn't immediately obvious what had killed them. There was no visible damage to their bodies but as he got closer, he could see that the wolves had been shot. He walked up to each one and examined it. Each wolf had a small hole in their body and another one in their head.

Blackwolf sat down and laid his head on his paws as he mourned their deaths. His entire wolf pack had been killed. Their deaths caused not by wolf. But by man. He became overwhelmed with emotion then sat up and howled louder than he ever had. It was mid-day but he howled like the bright light of the moon was shining down in the forest. As though the light was cast onto his beautiful shiny black hair. His howl was deep, painful and echoed throughout the valley. The trees, although plentiful, did not muffle his cries as residents came out of their homes and shop owners came out of their shops. Many of the residents who heard it called into the sheriff's office out of fear. Grant took many of the calls and then told Marguerite that he didn't want to take any more. He tried to calm the callers about the loud howl that seemed too close for comfort. *Dammit. I have to get a handle on this wolf problem,* he said, unaware that someone had beat him to it.

Giselle heard the wolf's howl and went to her window. It was a sad, depressed and lowly howl. One from an animal in deep pain and anguish. She instantly became sad and then angry. "Beth I'm leaving. I have to make a run. I'll be back. Forward my calls," she said. Giselle got in her car and drove to her house and changed into something more comfortable.

The howling still resonated the land. Giselle put on jeans, a tee shirt, covered it with a plaid button up shirt and put on her converse. She grabbed her Smith & Wesson, her 480 Ruger, her shotgun and Weatherby Rifle and headed out the door. She wasn't sure what she'd encounter but she knew she needed to go. She felt compelled to go. She hadn't seen the wolf or any wolves for that matter. Rumor around town was that the men of the town didn't feel comfortable hunting the wolves and had called off their kill searches. The men had told other residents that they had not killed any wolves. And so if that were true, what was causing a wolf to howl mid-day, on a sunny afternoon. A howl usually reserved for pain or mourning. Something was wrong. Giselle knew that the packs never did that out of fear of causing attention to themselves. The wolves rarely if ever, howled during the day and for such a long time. Giselle had a sinking feeling and wanted to go check things out for herself.

Giselle went to her garage and pulled out her ATV and started it up. She grabbed two gas cans and shook them. "Damn. Not even half full," she said about one of the cans, as she placed them in the back compartment making sure the lids were on tight. Giselle got on and drove towards the woods at the vehicles top speed as she navigated her way through the tough terrain. She looked around and fearlessly continued on her journey with one gun in her front waist and the other on her back. She drove for over twenty minutes looking around and heard the howling start again. She was able to pinpoint where it was coming from and drove north west up a hill until she came to snake river and stopped.

"Damn. I can't get across that. There has to be something," she said. Giselle drove down a few yards until she came across a manmade bridge that looked damaged but sturdy. She vaguely remembered the bridge. Her father had brought her to the very spot she was at and he fished in the river while Giselle played nearby. Her father was a skilled outdoorsman and knew how to avoid danger and was always prepared for it. Giselle learned what she could about animals, guns and the wild from him. She learned to respect all life but that she would need to protect herself from harm. To always be prepared with the most powerful weapons necessary.

The river had a strong current and it was rumored to be deep. So, she grew concerned and thought for a moment about turning back. She took a deep breath and then rode across it slowly. The bridge seemed weak and Giselle regretted her choice. The ATV shook violently as it hit the uneven and badly damaged planks. "Please hold firm," she said, as she tried to navigate the ATV. Once on the other side she picked up the pace and was shocked to see Alonzo sitting on a large stump. He had his head in his hand and never looked up at her as the engine from her ATV was loud enough to hear.

She stopped a few feet away from him and got off the ATV and looked around. She was shocked and speechless. He was surrounded by dead wolves, Giselle looked at the carcasses. She was saddened and could see that they all had some type of head wound, like an execution. "Alonzo. What are you doing? Why are you here?" she said, as she knelt down in front of him and tried to look him in his eyes. He wouldn't allow her to move his hands from in front of his face. Giselle sighed then looked around again. She looked back at Alonzo and rubbed his hand hoping he would say something to her.

"You want me to go get shovels so we can bury them in a big hole. Or we can burn them I have gas," she said, realizing that she didn't use her gas yet and had two cans. "No. I can do it. You need to go home," he said. "No. I'm not leaving here unless you go with me," she said, still trying to see him eyes. She could see he had tears on his face and was probably embarrassed. "Come on Alonzo," she begged. "No Giselle," he said.

Giselle got up and sat next to him on the log and put her arms around him. "You want me to go get some other men to help out," she said. Alonzo paused and sighed then replied *yes*. Giselle hugged him and stood in front of him. "There are dangerous animals out here. This is deep in. This is where they live. You want one of my guns for protection," she said.

Alonzo removed his hands from his face and stared at her. "No," he replied. "Ok. Um. Well I'll go back," she said. Alonzo reached out and grabbed her hand, held it for a minute then let her go. Giselle walked away slowly as he watched her. She looked back then got on her ATV and turned around. She hated to leave him. She wanted to comfort him. She wanted to hold him and help him through his pain. And tell him that she had been thinking of him nonstop and had been looking for him.

She looked back at him once again as she drove back towards the river. He was obviously involved with the wolves, but she wondered to what extent. Did he raise them? Was he their caretaker? Was that why the large black wolf that saved her appeared to be domesticated. Was Alonzo the reason.

This is how he got shot. What is he doing out here in this part of the woods? Hunters come in this deep looking for Elk and Deer. And who killed all those wolves. Where is the black one? I still haven't seen it, Giselle thought, as she drove away.

Giselle drove back across the bridge and made it to the other side and started her journey back when she stopped her ATV and was instantly paralyzed with fear. She grabbed her rifle and readied a shot for the massive 1300 pound Kodiak Bear in front of her. "Oh no," she said, as she teared up from fear. "Go the other way. Go. Please... Turn now. Walk the other way. I don't want to shoot you," she said, as the bear neared. The bear swung its front paw and Giselle fired a warning shot hoping it would scare the bear off.

She aimed her rifle at the bear and steadied her hand. She looked down the barrel and placed her finger on the trigger. Just as she prepared to take a shot, something moved swiftly through the dense vegetation. It was headed their way and it was moving at an astounding rate of speed. Giselle hadn't noticed as her anxiety had her holding the gun waiting for the bear to take another step. Out of the grass, the wolf leaped and ran past the bear. He moved swiftly, taking the bears left paw completely off. It was done with such ease, that Giselle wasn't sure what had occurred. The bear cried out then ran away in the opposite direction. Giselle barely got a look at the animal that attacked and only saw what looked like a black animal. She looked around ready to shoot whatever had done the damage to the bear and was shocked to see it was the black wolf. Her black wolf. She lowered her gun as he stood there looking at her.

Giselle got down off her ATV and slowly approached it. "Come here boy," she said holding her hand out. But it stood there. Giselle was thrown off by its behavior. It was normally friendlier with her. She walked up to it and rubbed the wolf on its head. "You're always there to save me huh," she said, as she smiled. She looked through the trees and across the river but no longer saw Alonzo. She saw the huge stump he had been sitting on but could not see him. She looked around as she rubbed the wolf on the head. Things weren't adding up but she didn't have time to go through it. Alonzo was somewhere on the other side of that river. He was waiting for her to return with men to bury the dead wolves. And so, she had to get going. "Ok boy. I have to go. I was worried about you," she said, as she walked away, glad he was ok. Giselle made it back and pulled into her shed and then went into her house. She immediately left back out headed into town and directly to the town's wildlife control office. Giselle walked in and spoke with a man. She wanted to explain what she had saw and hopefully get a team out to the location.

"There's a grieving man up near Snake River surrounded by about 15 dead wolves. Someone has massacred the wolves and he's up there alone. I believe some of them may belong to him. In any case, can you send a crew to bury the animals in a mass grave," she asked the man at the counter. "Ma'am... We have limited resources at the moment. We can't go right now, but we can try to go tomorrow," he said. "No. It has to be now. I was just there and I barely escaped with my life and I had four weapons on me. A bear tried to attack me and if it wasn't for this wolf, who knows what would have happened," she stressed. "What do you mean?" the man asked. "The wolf saved me. He bit the bears paw off. Took it completely off and the bear ran away," she said, as she looked seriously at him hoping what she said would spark a flame and get him to go.

"Ma'am... Was this a full grown bear?" he asked. "Yes," she replied, as her frustration grew. He looked at her curiously. "A large bear?" he asked sarcastically. "Yes. It was huge. I don't know. Maybe twelve hundred pounds or more. Huge," she replied. "Ok. ma'am, a lone wolf can't take a bears paw off in one bite. Ok. Their mouth is not big enough to accomplish that. They would have to work at it and chew it off and that would take some time," the man said, looking at Giselle with an expression that made her go into a full rant. "Are you calling me crazy. I know what I saw. The wolf is big too. He's huge. He's at least 7 feet, maybe two hundred and sixty pounds," she replied, biting her lip and angry that he didn't believe her.

"Ok ma'am... Wolves don't get that big. Have you been drinking?" he asked. "Oh, forget it. I'll go help him myself," she replied.

Giselle turned to walk away but the man called her back. The wildlife worker told her he and his men would go to the area prepared to dig a mass grave. He asked her to call the gentleman she knew and ask him to leave the dangerous area. That they would investigate and take care of it. Giselle asked if she could accompany them but the man told her he couldn't allow it. After arguing with the man back and forth, Giselle left out then tried to reach Alonzo. She knew it was a long shot since he was deep in the forest. She tried several times then walked to her car and sat there. *Why was he there? Why was he so affected? Are those his animals. Is that black one his too? What is going on?*

Giselle went back in and gave the man her number and pleaded with him to at least call her and tell her what happened and he agreed.

Giselle drove to the office walked in causing whispers amongst her coworkers. The jeans and disheveled appearance shocked everyone including Beth. "Everything ok Giselle," she asked. Giselle never wore jeans not even on dress down Friday. And her hair and make up weren't neat. "Yes. Hold my calls. I'm only here to look something up. I won't be here but a few minutes," Giselle said, as she went into her office and shut her door. She sat at her desk and researched *search and rescue* companies in the area. Her mind raced with thoughts of Alonzo. As she calmed down and thought about what she'd seen she had even more questions.

After checking for local rescue teams and not finding one close enough, she opened her emails. She saw her cell phone light up and answered. "Hi ma'am. This is Mark from the Animal &Wildlife office. We had a chopped in the area, surveying the land and he flew near Snake River. He was not able to locate your friend. Please tell me if you hear from him. Otherwise. We can't go until tomorrow," the man said. Giselle hung up from him and looked out the window. She thought she saw Alonzo but night was approaching and she couldn't see clearly. The man didn't look up at her the way Alonzo would have. Giselle wasn't sure. The man walked away and turned the corner. *Was that him?*

"Hey you got a minute," Beth said. "Sure," Giselle replied. She didn't really have any spare time but she liked Beth. "Come in," she said. Beth entered her office and shut the door. She looked distraught. "What's wrong," Giselle asked, concerned about the look on Beth's face. Something had happened. "I don't need to come over like we planned. He called off our date. Said he's having second thoughts. Just being mean and arrogant. I guess maybe I spooked him when I called a few times. He said I call too much. But I like him. I didn't think I was calling too much," she said, as she wiped her face. Giselle closed her laptop.

"Beth, I need to ask you something," she said. "Ok." Giselle waited then got straight to the point. "I have just one question. Have you ever slept with him? More importantly, have you slept with him since you bumped into him again?" she asked. "No. Never," she said. "Well then, you can never call him too much. That's bullshit. Where were you supposed to go?" she asked. "To the *Nightowl Lounge*," Beth replied. "Ok. Well. Then he's probably still going. He just wants to go alone. So were hanging out and that's where we're going. Let's see if he has seconds thoughts after Friday. I'm willing to bet he'll want to redeem himself," she said.

Beth smiled. "You think its ok. You don't think he'll feel like I'm stalking him," she said. "No cause you won't stalk him. When we go you say hi and you give him no more attention. Let him think about things," she said. Beth smiled and nodded and then looked intently at Giselle. "What's going on with you though. You seemed stressed when you first walked in," Beth said. Giselle looked at her and shook her head. "I am. It's weird Beth. Can I tell you something? And it stay between us?" she said. "Of course, Giselle. You know I don't talk to anyone," she assured.

"I think I'm falling for someone and I don't even know him like that. And I believe he feels the same way, but we just can't seem to come together. I don't know," she said, as she looked off. "He's probably making room in his life for you. Well at least that's what my father always said. He used to say that sometimes men had to make adjustments before they came to get the love of their life. Give him time. But be ready when he comes," she said. Giselle smiled at Beth. Beth was shy, awkward and didn't appear to be the type to be so well versed in relationships. Giselle liked her advice. It was dead on. It was exactly what she needed to do. Allow him to do what he needed to do and when he said *let's go*, she would be ready.

"Yeah. You're right. But back to you. Be at my house tonight," she replied. Giselle needed a distraction. Something to do. Her mind was racing with thoughts of Alonzo and he was an emotional wreck. And so, she needed to fill her time and give him time to grieve. She needed to follow Beth's advice, to the letter.

Chapter Nine - Elusive

Giselle went home and left her door open. She instructed Beth to come as soon as she could and they would get ready together. The plan was to go all out, get dolled up and then head over to the *Nightowl Lounge*. She sat her purse down then checked her voice mail and texts. She tried Alonzo's phone still hoping to talk to him. *Dammit. Where is he?* she stressed. She called the wildlife control office but got no answer. She wanted to tell them that she located him but that they still needed to go and bury the animals. She sat her phone down and walked to her window and looked out at the forest and became anxious. She wanted to tell Beth she had something pressing going on and would need to cancel. But she knew how important the night was to her and didn't want to disappoint her. *Where are you?* she said, as her feelings overwhelmed her. She wanted to go be with him.

Giselle walked away from the window and up the stairs. She turned the shower on and jumped in and exited after a few minutes. She dried off and put on her stretch pants and a tee shirt and waited for Beth. She walked to her front door and then back into her kitchen. Giselle saw her phone showing a missed call and dialed the unknown number back. "This is Mark," the man answered. "Hi this is Giselle calling you back," she replied. "Oh hi. I wanted to tell you that we went to the location. We didn't see your friend, but we did find signs of a mass grave. We pulled back some of the dirt and saw that it was a dead wolf so someone already dug it. It's a huge grave. A hole that size would have taken more than a day with at least four or more men. So, I'm not sure what's going on but, in any case, I wanted to update you." Giselle got worried. "No sign of him at all," she asked. "No Maam," he replied. "Ok. Well thanks for letting me know," she said, as she hung up and walked back to her window. *Where are you?*

Beth pulled up in awe as she admired Giselle home. It was more than she had pictured. The home was breathtaking. "Wow Giselle," she said as she pulled in front, right next to Giselle's Jeep. Beth got out the car and saw that the door was open. It was the perfect night to go out on the town. Beth was excited. She admired Giselle and would have never thought that she would be invited to her home. And that the two of them would be going out for a night on the town. She used to think of Giselle as a woman completely consumed with herself and unable to open up to anyone. Especially another woman. Beth felt special. Giselle had no other friends at the office and although she was nice and cordial, she didn't mingle.

"Hey. I'm here," Beth yelled, as she stood at the door. She walked up to her door and rang the bell. "Come on. It's open." Beth entered looking around in awe of her fabulous home. She was one of the executives. And so Beth had imagined she was living a wonderful, rich and exciting life. One filled with the best money could buy. "Come up here," she shouted from her room. Beth walked up the steps and into Giselle's massive bedroom.

"Wow Giselle. This is awesome," she said. "Thanks. It was my parents' home. My father and his friends built it. Then after my father sold his company for a lot of money, we moved to Canada. He had it updated then tried to sell it. No one wanted it at first because of the seclusion, the animals and I guess, the price. So he kept it. Then people started making him offers. I'm glad he kept it. I love this house. I love the land. The trees. Everything about it."

Beth sat on her bed and got comfortable. "Wow Beth. You look beautiful. And that dress... Ok So I'm going to do your makeup right quick then we are out of here," Giselle said, walking into her bathroom. Beth looked at the dress she had laid out. This is a nice dress. I love the color," she said. Giselle emerged from the bathroom with a tray of makeup and sat next to Beth. "Ok. Let's do something light. Did you bring your powder? My powder won't work on your skin unless you want to look like you been tanning," she said. "Oh yeah," she said, as she reached in her purse and pulled it out. Giselle took it from her and applied it to her face and started talking. She had a lot on her mind and was comfortable talking to Beth.

She liked Beth. Beth kept to herself. She was never in the middle of gossip or office whispers. Beth would do anything for her and even used to cover for her when she would sneak out of the office. She used to take long lunches to meet Grant for an afternoon romp and Beth never said a word. "I'm worried about the guy I told you about. He was out in the woods the last time I saw him and won't call me. I went there when I heard a wolf howling. I thought it might be this wolf I've kind of adopted. He's been domesticated and I kind of like him and was actually looking for the animal when I saw Alonzo," she said.

"This guy. He hangs deep in the woods? Is he a hunter?" Beth asked. "No. I don't know. Just a lot of things seem weird lately to me. Even Grant noticed and pointed it out to me. But I'm not trying to hear anything he has to say. But he's right. Strange things have been happening," she replied. "You know. I know an Indian by the name of Chitto. Do you know Chitto. He fixes cars. He lives east of here," she asked. "No. I don't think I know him. I've only been back in Kamiah for a few years."

Beth paused. "Well... He knows everything about wolves, bears, legends and this city's history. You should go talk to him. He even does readings. He'll look at you and tell you everything. I know it sounds weird but he's accurate. He's predicted my brother's wedding and how many kids he would have and I'll be damn if it didn't happen just like he said," she said. Giselle stopped applying her make up for a minute. "Where does he live?" she asked.

Beth told her what road Chitto stayed on and described where to turn. She told her to look for an old classic, rusted car with the words "Car Repair" spray painted on it. "Ok so look. I'm sure he didn't mean it the way you took it. So let's go out and he'll see you looking gorgeous and whatever he really meant, you'll see it tonight. But if it's not meant then you can't force it. Let's just go see. Men sometimes need to see a woman in her best light in order to get out their own way," Giselle stated. Beth smiled as she looked at herself in the mirror. "I thought I gave the best man advice. Wow!"

The women went to *Nightowl Lounge* and walked in. Beth saw her date Jason and walked by him, giving him a dry hi as her and Giselle walked by. Giselle looked at him and looked forward as his friends asked him who the two beauties were. "Hey Beth," Jason said, as he walked up to Beth. She and Giselle had already gone over what Beth was to do and say. Word for word. Blow by blow. "Jason," she said then looked around, ignoring him. "Sorry I couldn't keep our date. My buddies wanted to come out and I haven't seen them in a while so..." Beth looked at him and smiled and sipped her drink. "You want me to get you another," he asked. "No. After this we may go over to *Barney's*," she said, as Giselle chimed in. "Your friend in the blue is really handsome," she said, as Beth looked over. "Umhmm," Beth acknowledged. "Do your friends want to join us for drinks," Giselle asked. "Um. No. They're ready to play pool then I have to take Jeff home. He has to get up in the morning. "Oh too bad," Giselle said. "I meant to call you. See if you wanted to go out tomorrow instead," he asked.

Beth paused and smiled. "Tomorrows not good. But I'm free next Friday," she replied. "Um. Sure. You sure you don't want to go tomorrow," he repeated trying to get her to commit. Beth said she was sure and Jason paid for their drinks and then went to sit with his friends. Beth had Jason intrigued. Her dismissal coupled with the fact that she was beautiful, had him regretting his treatment of her. Beth was a natural beauty and she had a habit of downplaying her looks by going make up free and dressing in very homely ways. Giselle told her that men were visual. And so, it was part of their plan. To let him see Beth, dressed up and with natural, perfect applied make up. "Yep. Just like what we said. He just needed to see me again. Looking my best and not desperate to see him," Beth said. "Yep," Giselle replied, taking a sip of her cocktail.

Giselle and Beth decided to leave early as planned. They were escorted to their car by Jason, and the three laughed and walked through the parking lot. Jason's friend came out drunk and acting totally belligerent. "Heyyy. Get back here. Where you think you're going," he shouted. "Ignore him. Get in the car. He's drunk," Jason explained. The women rolled their eyes as the friend approached, loud and belligerent. "Jeff. Chill man," Jason warned. "I'm just talking. I'm just being friendly. Huh beautiful," he said, pulling on Giselle's arm. "Hey," she said, as she snatched away and looked at Jason. "Jeff. Enough man," he said. "What," Jeff continued. He walked up to Giselle and hugged her and pulled her close to him. "You are so fucking beautiful. You should come with us. Come on," he said. "No! I can't. I'm sorry. Not let me go. We're leaving," she replied. "Aw naw. Come on. We can take you home. Come on. The party just started," he said, as Jason tried pulling him back towards the bar. "Come on Jeff. Leave them alone," Jason said. "Move man. Get off of me. These bitches is stuck up. The pretty ones always too good to party. You think you're too good for us. Is that what this is," he said, as he pulled Giselle toward him and wouldn't let her go. "Jason get your friend before I hit him in the head," Beth warned. Giselle was getting angry as well. He was holding onto her tight and hurting her arm. "Let me go now," Giselle screamed.

Just as Giselle struggled to get free Alonzo came from out of the darkness. Beth saw him approaching, but Giselle was too busy trying to get free to notice him. "Let her go or I'll break your fucking arm," he warned. Giselle smiled when she saw him. Alonzo kept his eyes on Jeff never blinking and counting down the seconds he had left. Jeff let go of Giselle and Jason pulled him by the arm. Never taking his eyes off Alonzo who looked angry enough to destroy an army of men. Jason, fearful and not wanting any part of Alonzo's wrath, pulled Jeff by the arm back toward the bar. "Come on man," he said, as the men went back inside the bar.

"Giselle who is that?" Beth asked. "That's him," she said, smiling at Alonzo. "Beth this is Alonzo. Alonzo, that's Beth," she said. "Get in your car and go home Giselle," Alonzo said. Giselle walked up to him and got in his face. "Why every time I see you, you're always giving me orders," she said. Beth smiled. Alonzo was more handsome than she pictured. "Because you're always doing something," Alonzo replied, smiling at her.

"I've been looking for you. Where's your car?" Giselle asked. "It's close," he replied. "Good. Then I can go with you. You don't mind do you Beth," she said, as she looked at Beth. "You need to go with her. I have somewhere to go," he hesitated, not wanting to upset her. But Giselle instantly got upset. She didn't understand him. He was giving mixed signals and she wasn't sure why. Was he married? Did he care for her at all? She wondered if he felt any of the sparks between them and if he did, why wasn't he being more aggressive in pursuing her.

Giselle was disappointed and turned and walked to Beth's car. "Um. Nice to meet you," Beth said, confused at their intense but strange interaction. "You ok?" she asked when she got in the car. "No. Just take me home." Giselle didn't have much to say on the ride back to her house. Beth tried to change the subject and make small talk. But Giselle was quiet and emotional and looking as though she was ready to cry.

Alonzo had his reasons for keeping his distance. He couldn't risk her coming on to him because he knew he would not be able to control himself with her. He didn't trust himself with her. In order for the curse to be broken she had to tell him she loved him first. Then they could make love. And in that order. She couldn't think it and she couldn't say it to someone else. Giselle needed to say it to him, without the knowledge that a curse even existed. Their union had to be pure.

The next day Giselle woke up with a headache and still upset that Alonzo wouldn't allow her to go with him. She laid on her couch watching tv and twirling her hair in her fingers as she thought about him. She laid there stressed and anxious. She wanted to get in her car and drive to his home and tell him how she felt. That she liked him, maybe even loved him and she wanted him.

She was disappointed at what was becoming an obsession for her. Giselle had never wanted a man as much. She was lost as to why it seemed he felt the same. Why was there a problem coming together? He had already told her he lived alone. There was no wife. He turned her on an she hadn't had sex in a while. She had cut Grant off, since meeting Alonzo and that fact surprised her. In the past, she would have sex with Grant when she got horny and needed him sexually. But she was unable to bring herself to even consider Grant. She could only see herself with him. A man she hadn't even been with before. Giselle believed he was her soul mate. Only a soul mate would have such power over her without so much as a kiss. Giselle closed her eyes and imagined him and again got aroused. She kept her eyes closed as she felt strong sexual feelings all over her body. Giselle squirmed and then opened her eyes and looked around. *I'm suffering here. I can't sleep with Grant and Alonzo doesn't want me like that. Great!*

"Hi. Is the Sheriff in. My name is Mark Stiles. I'm from wildlife control," he said. Marguerite radioed Grant. "Sheriff Ellis," she said. "Yeah," he replied. "There's a gentleman here by the name of Mark Stiles. Says he's from wildlife control and he needs to talk to you," she said. "Ok. I was on my way back," Grant replied. "Have a seat. He's on his way back," she replied. The man sat down and waited on Grant to arrive.

After ten minutes Grant walked in and greeted Mark. "Hey man. Haven't seen you in a while," he said. "Yeah. I just need a minute of your time," he said. Grant and Mark walked into his office and Grant shut his door. "So how can I help you," Grant asked.

We had a complaint in our office about a massacre of wolves and went to investigate. When we got there, we saw a mass grave and moved some of the dirt and saw that there were animals in it. My concern is, that the witness said she saw at least 15 dead wolves and we count that there are twenty wolves in Wallowa Forest, all being tracked with embedded tracking devices in them. We personally caught and tagged twenty wolves. The wolves we tagged are between five and five and a half feet, hundred and fifty pounds at the most. The witness said she saw one that was seven feet and two hundred fifty pounds. I didn't believe her. But then I looked into some of the complaints and I believe she saw something, I just don't know what.

I don't believe she saw a wolf. Wolves usually don't take down the type of prey that has been reported to have been killed. One was a full-grown male lion at the Kamiah Zoo. It would have taken multiple, extremely large wolves to take him down. Plus, wolves don't attack lions. They're smart. They know the lion can injure many of them before they disabled it and they wouldn't risk losing members unless they were starving, which they are not. There are plenty of elk and deer. As a matter of fact, our elk and deer population has grown. And then there's a huge Kodiak Bear, dead on the

Beltway. It just doesn't make sense. Something else is killing the animals, but I don't know what, Mark stated.

"I don't think it's an animal. I believe it's a man. And that same man killed Steve Mitchell," Grant stated. Grant sat back in his chair. "Who filed the complaint?" he asked. "Oh. Uh. A woman named Giselle Jackson." Grant bit his lip. "She went in the forest?" Grant asked. "Yes. I believe so. It was just as she described. She said a man she knew was there and asked if we could rescue him. That he was in danger. We were shocked she even made it there. I mean. We didn't locate the site until we were many miles in. But when we got there, there was no man around," he replied. "The man she went to see is the man killing livestock. He has also killed one of our residents and he must be stopped, even if I have to use deadly force. He is armed and dangerous."

Chapter Ten - Legends

Giselle pulled up to Chitto's house. It was situated just as Beth had described and she looked around at the children playing. She smiled as the children played baseball with a stick and an old tattered ball. Chitto was bending over trying to lift a heavy piece of wood when he saw Giselle. He dropped it and walked down his driveway toward her car. Giselle got out of the car. She was dressed plain and comfortable in cut off jeans and a tunic.

"Hi I'm sorry to come to your home unannounced. My car is fine. I'm not here to get my car fixed. I wanted to talk to you about strange things that have been happening to me. I was told you see things. That you may know what is happening to me," she said, as she held her hand up above her eyes to block the sun. "You're the one that a spiritual war is brewing over," he said. "What," she replied, looking puzzled. "The sheriff came here. He wants to remove his enemies so that you'll consider him for marriage. He has killed in order to win back your approval. But he is up against a mighty warrior and he will continue bumping his head against him like a brick wall until he destroys himself. You have been marked. Do you own a wolf?" he asked.

"No. But one comes to see me. He has befriended me and has saved my life twice," she said. "That is the warrior. Your warrior. You belong to him. He has marked you," Chitto said. "What? What do you mean? What is marked?" Giselle asked. "He has imparted with your spirit and now you are one." Giselle was still not clear on what Chitto was saying. "How would I be marked? By feeding it and petting it? Is that why things keep happening to me?" she asked.

Chitto didn't want to scare her or give her too much detail. He believed that the spirit of the wolf would haunt him forever, if he divulged anything that would destroy its bond with what it marked. But he wanted to tell her enough so that she wouldn't fear what was happening and embrace it. Chitto looked at it as a gift and considered her lucky. "You would have been marked as a young girl. You encountered this wolf as a young girl and it marked you then. Two hundred and forty moons ago," he replied. Giselle's eyes got big and Chitto smiled. He could see that she remembered the mark. "Thank you for your time," she said.

Giselle walked back to her car and pulled off. She drove slowly as her mind raced. *That couldn't be the same wolf. The one from the forest when I was ten? The one that licked me on the face when my father was ready to shoot it? The one that I saw again before we moved? Was that wolf all black with a white... Yes... Yes... It was. Oh my!*

Days went by and Giselle longed for Alonzo. She went by his house under the guise of needing more information but he didn't answer the door. She was deeply saddened by his abrupt departure and requested vacation time to get herself together. She stared into the woods every evening hoping to see the wolf or Alonzo. He liked the woods and his home was just a mile up from hers. He had been in her tree before, she was sure of it. He was the man that she saw and he would not be able to convince her otherwise. She didn't care if he was in her trees. She welcomed him to sit in them, if it made him feel close to her. She knew he had feelings for her and she was still puzzled as to why he couldn't just come out and say so.

Giselle had emotionally distanced herself from Grant. He continued making himself available to her, cutting her grass and chopping wood for her. Giselle noticed she hadn't had any spontaneous orgasms since Alonzo was gone and began to wonder why. *Are my feelings for him that strong that I was making myself have orgasms?* she wondered. She welcomed them. They were powerful and she enjoyed having them. But she wanted one with him. She wanted Alonzo and she decided that she would wait for him. *I know you're coming back to me,* she thought, as she stared out the window.

Alonzo was filled with fury and now determined to destroy his enemies. Grant was plotting to kill him. And Darius was plotting to stop his love affair with Giselle and ultimately destroy any chance of him breaking the curse. Darius' actions had caused Alonzo to constantly change into Blackwolf for his pack family and Alonzo had five months to break his curse or he would remain a wolf forever. Darius believed Alonzo would not break his curse. He was staying close enough to Giselle to know that Alonzo was not spending real time with her. He watched and listened as she cried her eyes out to Beth about not being able to see Alonzo. Now with Alonzo's entire pack dead, Darius rejoiced because part of his plan worked. The humans had blamed Alonzo for the slaughter's and had hunt his pack down.

But Darius still had one more problem. Alonzo was still alive. He couldn't kill him. He wasn't powerful enough. He needed the humans to finish what they started and kill him. Darius was afraid to go after Giselle again. That was him the night she had the flat tire. The night Alonzo attacked him and then escorted Giselle home. He knew if he went after her again, Alonzo would abandon all reason and kill him and his entire pack.

Darius also knew not to destroy Alonzo's entire pack because Alonzo would then be free to stay in human form and be available to Giselle. But when someone destroyed Alonzo's pack, even though it caused him great pain, it freed him. He was now free to change into Blackwolf when he wanted versus being forced to, in order to protect the family. And he could now strike Darius without fear of retaliation. Darius knew he had to now change his plans. The only way to prevent Alonzo from breaking his curse would be to incite the humans or destroy Giselle. He had nothing to lose. Darius was willing to take that chance. He hated Alonzo and he hated himself. He didn't want to be a wolf for the rest of his life. And so, he was ready to make another move. He would rather die than watch Alonzo live free

"Hey Beth," Giselle said, as she walked in and up to the receptionist station. "Hey. You been ok?" Beth asked. "Yeah girl. I'm only going to be here for a few hours. I'm going to keep working from home. I may take a leave from here and just work on everything from home," she said, in a melancholy, somber voice. Giselle and Beth had talked outside of work and so Beth was aware that Giselle felt overworked, stressed and confused about her strong feelings for Alonzo. "Do what you need to do until you get yourself together. I can help you. I'll do all your follow ups if you need me to," Beth offered. Giselle smiled.

Beth had turned out to be a good and trustworthy friend and she was grateful for any help she could get. She knew Beth didn't understand what was actually troubling her. She barely understood it herself. She had a sadness of unknown origin that she couldn't wrap her head around. And the person with the answers was missing in action. "Thanks Beth. I'll let you know if it becomes too much to take on. You seen Mr. Garner yet? Is he in his office?" she asked. "Yes. He just got in not too long ago," she replied. Giselle walked back to his office and slowly walked in. He held his finger up in a *hold on* gesture as he finished up with a client.

Giselle stood and waited as he wrapped up his conversation. "Giselle. You ok? I've been worried," he asked, looking concerned. Giselle was the company's powerhouse. He was hoping that by giving into all her special request, that she was getting back focused. He was hoping that she would be prepared to get back to her responsibilities at the office. Not working in the office meant that she wasn't around for last minute fixes. That she wouldn't be there to help out in a crunch on projects that were past the due date. "I'm ok but I still would like to continue working from home. I came in to work just a few hours and help out but I would like to take a month off. Maybe come in as needed, to work on late projects. I'm just not ready to return," she said.

Mr. Garner paused and weighed his words carefully before speaking. He wanted to retain her services as an employee due to her impeccable reputation and work ethic. He didn't want to say anything that may be misconstrued. He valued her and knew her worth. And unlike a lot of CEO's he understood that if he didn't support her now, he could lose her later.

"Look Giselle. I'm not sure what's going on but you are a very valuable member of this team. If you need another month then you got it. But I hope it won't be much longer than that. I wouldn't want the company to start suffering due to your absence. Andy has taken on a lot to cover for your absence but he is starting to show signs of stress. He's used to you having his back. You know what I'm saying. But your own work hasn't suffered so if it's a month you need, you got it," Mr. Garner stated.

"Yes. Just another month," she assured. Giselle and Mr. Garner talked about projects, new clients and prospective clients. She agreed to help land some of the new customers and to work on their more difficult projects. She got up and left out of his office, walking past Beth and shaking her head. Beth acknowledged the look and continued with the call she was on. She knew that look was a show of her own discontent for whatever ailed her. Giselle walked towards Andy's office and walked in.

"Hey Cyber," she said, as she walked over to his desk. "GiGi. The goddess of the web," he playfully said smiling at her. "Hey listen. I'm sorry I haven't been around. If you need help getting through some of the projects you can email them to me. I didn't mean for this to dump on you," she said. "Gi. I got this. I can do this stuff with my eyes closed. As long as them checks keeps rolling, I'm good," he said.

Andy was a handsome, skinny, nerdy looking computer whiz and he adored Giselle. He never tried to come on to her. He didn't think she was attracted to him and never wanted to be in an awkward position with her so he kept his attractions to himself. He didn't think she had ever dated a white guy and so that, coupled with the fact that he knew she was involved with their Sheriff, kept him from exposing his feeling for her. "You ok though," he asked. "Yeah. Just personal issues. Women stuff," she said, smiling at him. "Oh geez. Say no more. I got you," he said. "Thanks," she said, as she turned around and walked out of his office.

Giselle went to her office and opened her emails and scanned them looking for her priority messages. She went through them then checked her itinerary. She looked off and then over at her window. Thoughts of Alonzo entered her mind and she looked back at her messages. She opened a web construction application and opened an old file. She began working on an intricate and extensive web page for a large company with specific needs. She worked on their web page for two hours then shut her computer down and talked to Beth for a few minutes before leaving for the day.

Giselle drove home and as she approached her street made a quick decision to go to Alonzo's house. She pulled into his private road and drove toward his home looking through the trees at his home as she got closer. She pulled up in front and put her car in park and got out, leaving her car running. She walked up to the door and knocked, then looked over and glanced inside. She rung his doorbell and knocked and waited as she looked around.

What if he's here? What will I say? I look like a stalker. Giselle just go home, she thought, as she stood there on his porch. There were no signs of him and Giselle sighed then walked off his porch and got back in her car. Giselle was unaware that lurking in the thick bushes near the trees on the edge of his driveway was Darius. He had been following her and stalking her. She was just minutes from him exiting the bush and attacking her. Giselle looked back at Alonzo's front door once more before pulling off.

Giselle went home and slung off her shoes and immediately walked to her kitchen. She grabbed an apple from her fruit basket and went into the living room. She was strangely quiet and unsociable. She turned her colleagues down for after work drinks, even after Beth stated she was going. Giselle was becoming withdrawn. She wanted nothing and no one except Alonzo. She was now off of work indefinitely while she tried to get some sort of normalcy back in her life. She laid down across her couch and grabbed her remote. She cut the tv on but turned her head and closed her eyes. She glanced at the television but struggled to keep her eyes open. Her eyes felt heavy. She was fatigued. She was exhausted. As hard as she tried to stay up, sleep won.

Darius crept up to the house. Giselle laid there asleep as he watched her through her window. He stood at her back glass sliding door. He wished there was a way to enter her home and kill the love that was destined to save his cousin from the same fate as he. Darius stared for several minute then trotted off into the forest to locate his pack. His plans to destroy Giselle would have to be put on hold.

Giselle was an avid outdoors woman and did a lot of her own outside chores but not this day. She hadn't worked her grounds in over a week and it was starting to show. The grass was starting to look overgrown but Giselle was too distracted to do anything more. She was having a hard enough time keeping up with her companies demands. And she was doing everything in her power to stay away from Grant and refused to call him to ask for help.

As night fell, the sounds of crickets chirping and the hooting sounds of an owl resonated from the forest and surrounding land. Giselle jolted awake and went to her sliding door and opened it when she heard the howling sounds of wolves. The sound she heard was Darius' pack as they congregated together. They had been successful in the fresh kill of a deer and feasted on their evening meal. Giselle looked up in the sky as it was filled with clouds and a partially full moon lit the area. "I slept too long. Ok. Well. I'm not starting anything now," she said, as she realized she hadn't touched her project that was due in two days. She hadn't intended on sleeping so late into the evening. *Ok. I'll do it tomorrow. I'll work on it all day until its complete,* she thought. Giselle put off her work until the next day. She was in no mood to do anything and continued standing in her doorway looking out into the trees.

She began to have a sense of being watched again and stared with greater intensity. Blackwolf was closer than she thought. But was bothered by the scent of wolves all around Giselle's home, in particular, Darius'. It was high concentrations of his scent as if he had been camped out near her. He smelled the trees and shrubs and checked the perimeter of her house. He detected Darius' scent throughout most of the areas.

Giselle ran a bath and removed her clothes and got in the tub. She relaxed for a minute then washed and immediately got out. She put on her pink silk knee length nightgown and the matching robe and rubbed lotion on her legs, arms and neck. She rubbed herself slowly and deliberately as she tried to rub away the stress of her unfulfilled desires. She sat in her dimly lit room staring out the window and at her outdoor chairs and decided she wanted to be out versus in doors. She loved the night and it was a cool and beautiful night. The large porch built off her bedroom was a perfect resting spot to lay and soak up the night. She was tired but she needed to feel alive. Sitting in the house was getting depressing and she felt herself going stir crazy.

Giselle walked out on her bedroom porch with her extra-long lighter and lit her citronella candles that surrounded the perimeter. There was a bug zapper LED light hanging off to the side and the entire system, worked good at keeping the bugs away. Giselle laid down on her brown wicker chaise and stared at the sky. She felt as though she were wrapped in a blanket of serenity.

As she laid there, comfortable and relaxed, she realized it was the first time in days, she wasn't stressed about her thoughts of Alonzo. As if he was there. Something had her comforted in a way she hadn't felt in weeks. Her eyes began to get heavy again and she closed them allowing her surroundings to continue to bring her peace. Giselle fell asleep as Blackwolf switched back into human form and then watched her from the same tree he always watched her from.

He could not leave her side with her sleeping outside. Darius was lurking around her house probably with the intention of harming her. Alonzo had been on a hunt himself. He was looking for Darius since picking up his scent around Giselle's yard. He knew what Darius was up to and knew what he needed to do. His pack was one thing, Giselle was quite another. Alonzo sat perched, watching over her and protecting her from harm for hours. Giselle awoke when a strong gust of wind blew across her body, sending chills and causing her to shiver. She got up and dropped the tops on her candles to extinguish the fires and walked inside. She sat on her bed and stared out into the distance. Alonzo sat there for a moment, then jumped down out the tree and headed home. He walked with purpose as he made the painstaking decision that to keep her safe, he had to kill Darius.

"Just a second," Giselle yelled, as she heard knocking on her door. "Hey," she said, as she let Beth in. "Hey. I just came by to check on you. I'm on my way to my step mother's. Even though my dad passed away, we're still close. We're going to go shopping," Beth said. Giselle smiled and walked to her kitchen. She wished she had those moments of shopping with either of her parents. They had both passed away several years apart and she had no one left but distant relatives she didn't know very well. Beth had lost both her parents as well. But she had a stepmother that lived in

Craigmont that she still kept in contact with. Giselle's parents had her late in life and she was their most cherished possession. They lived, worked and planned for her life up until the day they died, leaving her financially sound and filled with wonderful memories.

"Can you fax these documents for me Monday morning when you go to work. No rush. I just need the client to sign off on the job and pay any remaining balances they owe," Giselle stated. "Sure. Otherwise, you good," Beth asked. Giselle shook her head no. "But I will be. I just need some time. I don't know why I'm so upset over him. We barely did anything. It's not like we were in a committed relationship," she said. "I'm going back to see that man Chitto. I went to see him after you told me about him. He knows something more. I could tell. There's something he's not telling me," Giselle said. "He knows everything," Beth assured.

Chapter Eleven - Amends

"Hey Marguerite. Sheriff Ellis here," the man asked, as he walked into the sheriff's station. "Yes he is. And how have you been sir? How's Mary," Marguerite asked of their longtime resident Jim Schaefer. "Oh. She's great. My grandkids are growing up. We got another one on the way," he said. "Wow. Well congratulations. Let me just check and see if he's busy," she said. Marguerite went in and then came back out of Grants office and left his door open. "Go right in Jim. He's free," she said. Jim walked into the office and sat down. "Sheriff Ellis. How are you?" he said. "Hey Jim. I'm good. So, what brings you here? Did you lose more livestock?" Grant asked. Jim was one of the first ones to have his cattle ripped to pieces and had warned Grant early on that something sinister was amidst.

"No. But I heard about Steve Mitchell. I wanted to help hunt those animals down. I have special bullets that will stop them. Those bullets your using won't work. I heard that you're using Black Talon's. Even those won't work. You need silver bullets," he said. Grant had heard about using silver bullets before but wasn't sure that was necessary. He had none in stock and he heard they were expensive to produce and would need to get them special made.

"I can't get silver bullets. I can't get approval for something like that," Grant replied. "I have them. I ordered them when I saw my cattle torn the way it was. That was no pack of wolves feeding. I been here all my life. I know what bear and wolf feedings look like. That was a slaughter. Probably by a lone animal of considerable size and power. How do you tear a cow in half? I want the thing dead and I'm willing to arm your men with the bullets they need to accomplish that. I heard you shot a black one and didn't kill it. That's the one that you'll need these bullets for," he advised.

Grant sat back and listened to Mr. Schaefer. He was torn between his love for Giselle and his responsibilities as sheriff. The pressure had been mounting ever since the death of the hunter Steve Mitchell. His wife had filed a multi-million dollar law suit and he was under pressure from the mayor. But Giselle had shut down on him and he believed his hunting for wolves was the reason. "Let me think about how we should proceed. A pack of wolves was eliminated already but there are more. I believe they're deeper in the woods. I have to decide if it's worth the risk. The animals are so far in, that we could have trouble trying to reach them. We only have so many hours of light and we have to be out of there by dusk. Plus, no other livestock have been killed since the elimination of the pack so I'm not sure it's necessary," Grant said. Jim sat up and stared at him. "That pack was killed with regular bullets. Those were regular wolves, smaller in size and not capable of what I saw. What you're looking for is huge. A mammoth sized animal more powerful than anything you've ever seen and it's out there still. That black wolf is what you need to hunt down," he replied.

"Hey listen... What about this new guy that's in town? The residents say he's a landscaper and builder. I haven't met him yet. I can't seem to run into him. You met him?" he asked. "Yeah. Alonzo. He a good guy. He did our neighbors yard. Built her a fabulous gazebo. He does great work. I'm thinking of hiring him myself to help me build a new hen house," he said. "Can you set up a meeting. I want to meet him," he said. "Sure. I'll set it up. I'll call you," he said, as he stood up and extended his hand.

"Thanks Jim," Grant said, as the men walked out of Grant's office. Grant watched as Jim left and then turned and walked back in his office and shut his door. Grant sat at his desk when his cell phone rang. He saw it was his sister Jeanine. She was coming into town to visit with him before traveling to Nevada. "Hey sis," he answered. "Grant honey. How are you. We're almost there," she said, referring to her and her husband Daniel. "Ok. Let me know when you're close and I'll meet you at the house," he said. Grant smiled as he hung up. He hadn't seen his sister in a year. She drove from Montana to see him and then drove to Nevada to visit with her husband's family. She had plans on staying with Grant for several days before continuing her travels.

Darius was in town but staying hidden keeping up with Grant by traveling from his house and to the station. His plan had already picked up steam as he heard Grants conversation with Jim Schaefer through Grants open window. The window sat off the back of the station facing the dense trees and shrubs just yards away. Darius knew that Alonzo had been blamed for the livestock slaughter. The slaughter that he was responsible for. And now he would be turning up the heat. If he could kill Grant, tearing him in half the same way he did the cattle, then Alonzo would be hunted down for sure. Jim Schaefer was a well-connected man and could get things moving if he put his foot down. His family had been instrumental in the towns progress and he was politically connected. His son in law was the current mayor and his eldest grandson was on the council board. Darius hid in the shrubs and waited. He was ready to strike that evening.

Giselle ran errands and was back home within an hour. She baked herself some chicken breast and steamed vegetables and sat at her kitchen table. She ate as she thought about the strange coincidences that still didn't make sense. Her visit with Chitto had only added to her confusion and she was ready to talk again. She had specific questions that she knew he had the answers to. There was a connection between the wolf that she had seen as a child and again as a teenager and she wondered what Alonzo's connection was.

Why was he in her trees? Why was he always in the forest and why did the black oversized wolf appear around the same time? Why did the wolf seem so attached to her? Why did Alonzo seem attached as well? She knew about folklore and legends but didn't hear of any specifically related to what she was experiencing. Giselle stared at the wall then jumped up and ran to her room and opened her laptop. She did a search for wolves. Then searched wolves and legends. She also did a search for her town and looked up local folklore and legends.

Giselle carried the laptop to her living room and sat down, resting her legs on her foot rest as she read page after page, article after article about wolves and women and legends. After four hours of intense reading and saving the information she wanted, she closed her laptop in disbelief. She was speechless. What she read couldn't be true. Giselle stared out into the wilderness. It all added up. It made sense even though no one would believe her. It had to be true. It was the only thing that fit. *I have to go see Chitto. I need more,* she said. She was desperate to talk to him but it would have to wait until the next day.

Giselle had no appetite. Her mind had raced all day and throughout the evening. She now had more answers, but she wasn't sure what was fact. What was fiction. Or what was actually related to her. She always thought that legends were the babblings and made up imaginations of people who liked to scare others by making up stories. Stories that were used to explain things that were just freakish in nature and one-time occurrences.

She sipped her tea and looked over her property and the land. She looked at the mountains and tall pine trees and over at the part of the lake visible from where she was standing. She had a better view of it when she was up on the second level of her home. But what she could see, at that moment, was breathtaking. The sun was a reddish orange color and was absolutely stunning as it disappeared over the horizon giving way to the evening sky. And as beautiful as her view was it did nothing to help the sadness that came over her. The thought that she would not see him again. He had come and gone like a beautiful gust of wind. This day was the hardest but Giselle tried to stay strong. She believed she had no right. He was not hers. She was not his. She was starting to believe that what she was feeling, was self-induced and not real. But it was real. It was real to her. She was in love.

Giselle walked away from the window again, in heavy thought about Alonzo and wishing she could see him. He was there. Again, as he usually was. He had to be to keep her safe and he wanted to feel close to her. But her behavior had begun to concern him. She seemed heavy hearted and hadn't been to work. And her thoughts of him had taken on a more worried tone. Her thoughts of him had increased and had intensified and he decided to surface so she would feel normal again. He had channeled her so much that she was unable to function without knowing if he was ok.

Alonzo walked slowly from the woods towards her house. He walked with purpose. His woman was in some slight distress and he needed to soothe her spirit. Giselle was laying across her couch and looking at messages from Beth describing her first date with Jason. A warm sensation came over her. She hadn't felt the feeling and she slowly sat up. *Oh no. Not another orgasm out of nowhere,* she said. But the feeling seemed muted. Not powerful enough to cause an orgasm but was nonetheless, soothing.

Giselle got up and walked to her window. Something was in the distance. She squinted to see what the shadowy figure was in the darkness and then lit up with joy when she saw it was Alonzo coming up her yard. *He's here*, she said, as she wiped her tears and opened her door. She stepped out, smiling as he approached, but her emotion got the best of her and she ran to him.

Alonzo reached his arms out and she jumped on him. He held her as she hugged him then laid her head on his shoulder. Her face lay on his skin. Her mouth against his neck. He could feel the warmth of her breath. Alonzo was overcome with emotion at how Giselle was expressing herself. He could tell she wanted him totally and completely.

"You been looking for me," he said, with a smile. Giselle looked down to catch her breath. She laughed at herself for doubting their bond. She teared up again, as her heart filled with joy that he was there. "Yes," she said. Alonzo grabbed her gently by the face and kissed her passionately. "I missed you so much," she said, as she continued kissing him. Alonzo lifted her as though she weighed three pounds and carried her inside her house. They kissed with a yearning desire that was the result of two people destined to be together. Their bond had turned into an obsession with one another. Giselle only knew that he was the one. She had nothing to tie that reality to, other than she longed for him and it had no explanation.

Alonzo carried Giselle up her stairs and into her room and laid her down. Her room was lit with half a dozen candles as if she knew he would be coming this night. Alonzo slowly removed his shirt as Giselle watched him and took in the sight of his magnificent body. He was muscular all over and was a visual work of art. Giselle's breathing increased as she anticipated every inch of him. If it wasn't for the fact that she considered herself somewhat of a good girl she would have swallowed his perfect and large penis whole. Just from the sheer sexiness of him. But Giselle allowed him to lay on her and immerse his tongue into her mouth in a slow and sensual way as she moaned and kissed him. Giselle pulled back. "Where have you been?" she asked. Alonzo paused as he rubbed the side of her face. "I had things to do. Things I can't tell you about now but I will," he said.

Giselle looked at him with curiosity. "Why can't you tell me now," she said. "Not now. But I will. Soon," he replied.

Alonzo kissed her and ran his warm fingers across her body. Giselle was enjoying the heat emanating from him. It was a warm and enveloping heat that seemed to touch her soul. Alonzo kissed Giselle on her neck and then made his way down her body slowly as she squirmed and panted. Every hot kiss he planted drove her mad. She clawed and scratched his back gently and lovingly waiting for him to continue his decent down her body. Alonzo smiled as he read her mind and her dirty thoughts.

He followed her mental instruction on where he should kiss her next. He followed her requests on what she wanted him to do to her. Every thought she had he indulged and when he got to her vagina, he felt her have an orgasm before he even touched it. Giselle grabbed his face and pulled him to her. He licked and sucked her with a mouth and tongue that was many degrees warmer and it caused her to come immediately.

Giselle moaned, squirmed then tried to muffle her screams with her pillow. She enjoyed every second he spent savoring her smell, taste, warmth and the sounds she made. Giselle began to have thoughts of him inside her. She was ready to feel him. She wanted to put him in her mouth first and then she wanted him inside her. Alonzo could not allow her to do either. He could not consummate their union. He could only enjoy her. She could not put him inside her until she verbalized that she loved him and that included her performing oral sex.

His father had consummated his relationship with Alonzo's mother Mirra and was doomed to remain a wolf forever. Darius' father didn't have sex with her until she told him she loved him. Alonzo was aware that he could not make love to Giselle and believed she loved him. But until she made it known, he could not be with her. Alonzo decided to give her multiple orgasms mentally as he had done many times before and orally until she was exhausted. They held and kissed each other through the night until Giselle fell asleep in his arms. As Giselle lay sleeping, Alonzo watched her as if she would disappear. He never took his eyes off of her.

She was the most beautiful woman he had ever seen and he stayed up throughout the night watching her sleep.

Giselle stretched her arms the next morning and woke to an empty bed. "Oh no. Not again. Where did he go now?" she said, as she jumped up. She ran down her stairs and on her table was a note that read: *Will be back tonight. Had something to do.* Giselle smiled and walked back up her stairs and got back in her bed. She was unable to sleep as she almost had another orgasm, thinking about her wonderful and exciting night with him. She wished she had made love to him but she was satisfied. He was way beyond what she thought a lover could be. She was officially in love with him and would wait patiently for his return.

She looked over at the clock and decided she had enough time to get dressed and go to work. Even though she still had weeks before she needed to return, she decided it would make her day go by faster, if she went in. *I'll go in to work for a few hours. Then, I'll go get us something for dinner tonight,* she thought, as she got out of bed and headed to her bathroom.

"Good morning Beth," Giselle said, grinning from ear to ear. "Ok. Wait. First... What are you doing here? And second, I know that look because I had a similar one my face last night," she said. "Wouldn't you like to know," Giselle teased. Beth smiled and got up and followed Giselle into her office. "He showed up? Right? Only the mystery man could make you this happy," Beth exclaimed.

Giselle shut her door and pulled Beth by her hand toward her desk so no one could hear their conversation. "Ok. So, he shows up, middle of the night. Carried me in my house and into my room and the rest, well I can't tell you. Because you'll be looking for him yourself," she said, as Beth laughed. "What! Was it like that?" she asked. "Yes bitch. Better," she replied. Beth burst into laughter. "You better give me details. I can handle it. What?" she said. The women talked for a half hour about Alonzo and Jason, with excitement as they listened to each other stories.

Beth went to her desk briefly to send a fax and respond to a few calls. She then put the phone system on unavailable so that callers would be forced to enter the extensions they wanted. Or go into voice mail. Beth hurried back into Giselle office and saw her mood had changed slightly. "What's wrong?" she asked. "Oh Beth. I know nothing of him really. I moved so fast and I don't even know why. I have never moved that fast. I made Grant wait months and here I am, already way past the point of no return. I am totally gone over him and I haven't even fucked him," she said.

"What? I thought you said you did," she said, confused and sure she heard Giselle say he was awesome in bed. "We did. I mean. Well. He did… You know," she said. "No I don't know. What?" Beth said, looking curiously at Giselle. "He went down on me. Like all night. Like literally until I was in a coma. And has the biggest, scariest, prettiest looking dick ever. I have no idea how I'm supposed to fuck it but I'm going to figure it out," she said, smiling. "Why didn't you fuck him last night," Beth asked.

Before Giselle could respond, CyberMaster walked in. "What's up GiGi. Need you to finish the Milliken account. I am tied up adding a million upgrades to the Davis account," he stressed. Giselle took the file from him and he closed the door as he left. "I don't know Beth. He didn't even try. And I planned on it this morning. I wasn't going to let him get away without us doing it and he was gone when I woke up," she said, looking away and appearing to be in deep thought. "Maybe he can't. Maybe it don't work," Beth replied. "Oh it works. It felt like a pipe. Something else is going on."

"Hey," Grant said, as Jeanine got out of the car and eagerly hugged her big brother. Grant kissed her on the cheek and shook his brother in law Daniels hand then helped carry in their bags. Grant had a nice, large, four bedroom ranch home on 2 acres of land that he kept meticulous. "Where's Giselle?" Jeanine asked, as she walked in. "Um. She's around. She's been tied up lately. Work commitments," Grant replied.

Grant thought of her and was saddened for a moment. He hadn't talked to Giselle, but had tried to stay close to where he thought she was. All in hopes of getting a chance to see Alonzo. He had been following her around when he was free but hadn't any luck running into Alonzo. He had grown frustrated because he had yet to catch a glimpse of the man. Jim Schaefer, the resident who had silver bullets, had been unable to get in touch with Alonzo. And so Grant was back at square one.

"Are you guys good?" Jeanine asked, referring to his and Giselle's relationship. She knew her brother and noticed his mood change. "Oh yeah. We're good," he said. Jeanine gave him a look. She grabbed her duffle bag and walked to the bedroom she usually stayed in. Grant and Daniel stayed in the living room and talked about current events. Daniel was an officer of the law in the state of Montana and so they always had plenty to talk about. Work or sports was a consistent conversation for the brother in laws. Jeanine came back out and sat on the couch next to her husband and the three of them planned to go out to eat at a local five-star steak house later in the evening.

Giselle completed her work and left after meeting with Mr. Garner. She made a stop at the grocery store then stopped at a road side vegetable stand. "Hey Clarice," she said, as she approached. "Hey Giselle. What do you need?" she asked. "I'll take some squash, potatoes, carrots and broccoli," Giselle replied, looking around. As she walked over to the tomatoes, she heard a car pull up.

Grant was on his way to the sheriffs' station and saw her car. "Giselle," he called out. She looked at him and gave him a forced smiled as she looked around. She didn't hate him but his presence was not welcomed. Not if he was there to ask where they went wrong and if she would give him another chance. Giselle hated to hurt his feelings but there would be no more chances. There was a new sheriff in her town and she was in love with him. "Hey Grant," she said. "Hey. Jeanine is here. She asked about you," he said, hoping she would ask to see her. Jeanine and Giselle had become instant friends and spoke whenever they could, through email or texts.

"When did she get here?" she asked. She adored Jeanine and even though her and Grant weren't together, she wanted to see her. "Today. We're going to dinner tonight. She's only here for a few days. You want me to bring her to you," he asked. Giselle instantly shot down that idea. Alonzo was coming back and she wouldn't dare have him bump into Grant.

"No. But I'll come see her. What time are you going to dinner?" she asked. "Tonight. Around Nine," he replied. "Ok. Well. I'll be there before you go to say hi to her," she said smiling. "I miss you Giselle. Don't you want to go with us," he asked, hoping again to hear the words yes. "I don't think so Grant. I'm involved with someone. As a matter of fact, this is probably a bad idea. I think I'll call her and meet her for lunch. I really don't want to be around you. I'll never forgive you for killing and entire pack of wolves like that. What kind of human being are you?" she said, as she slowly shook her head at him. "Is that what you think. I didn't do that Giselle. Yes. I got a kill order approved, but we never found them. And besides, I would have never killed pups. We would have delivered them to a sanctuary to be raised and cared for," he said.

Grant was heartbroken. She had blamed him for something he didn't do and now it was too late for him to fix it since she now loved someone else. "Well, can you at least stop by to see Jeanine. She will be disappointed if she leaves and hasn't seen you," he said. "I will," she said. Giselle watched him as he walked back to his car and Alonzo watched her from a distance. He was led there by Darius' scent. He had been tracking Darius who was following Grant. He had no idea he would bump into Giselle. Alonzo was jealous that they had spoken but he read her mind and saw she was not emotionally attached to Grant and had in fact, told him she was seeing someone. But Alonzo also read jumbled and confusing thoughts on a possible visit to Grants house. He assumed she was going there for a final hook up. Her thoughts did not go to Jeanine but was stress related thoughts regarding Grant. Alonzo left the area since Darius was nowhere in sight. He went home, upset that she was still involved, to some extent, with Grant.

Darius was trying to stay two steps ahead of Alonzo. He could tell that Alonzo had been tracking him. He had doubled back to Giselle's home just to watch her movements. He could smell Alonzo's scent around the perimeter just as Alonzo had picked up his scent. He had also picked up his scent near Grants home. In their wolf form, things like vision, sense of smell, hearing and speed were increased many times more than in human form. And the scents smelled different. Alonzo's human form scent smelled different that his Blackwolf scent. And Darius could tell that he had been tracking him in wolf form, probably to attack him. So, his time was limited. It was obvious that Alonzo was coming for him.

Grant went to his office and stayed for a few hours then went back home to entertain his sister and her husband. He had relayed the message that Giselle would be coming to visit before they went out to eat. "Grant. Be honest. Tell me what's going on between you and Giselle," Jeanine said. Grant hesitated but then opened up and told her how he felt and what was happening between them. "We're not seeing each other right now. She told me she's seeing someone so I'm just letting her have her space," he said. "Aw Grant. I'm sorry I know you loved her. Maybe she just needs some time," she replied, concerned about his feelings. She knew he was in love with Giselle and had even talked of marrying her one day. "Yeah. I guess," he said in a low voice. Grant grabbed the remote and turned the tv on then grabbed his cell phone. He called Giselle to see if she would be on her way soon. Jeanine watched a movie as she waited for Giselle to arrive and for time to pass so they could go get something to eat.

"Hey, it's me. You coming," he asked. "Yeah I'll be there soon," Giselle replied. She had been looking out the window for Alonzo to show up. He had promised her he would be back but hadn't showed up. She considered running to Grants home for a few minutes then racing back. That way she would be home when he showed up. *Damn. Where is he,* she said, as she sat her phone down and walked to her window. She had glanced out of the window more than a dozen times looking for him. Another hour had passed and there was still no sign of him. Giselle grabbed her shoes and headed out the door. *He's doing another disappearing act,* she thought, as she walked to her car and got in. Giselle drove over to Grants house, talking to herself and getting angrier by the minute. "He's not going to keep doing this. This is a definite sign that he's unstable. I can't get involved if he's going to do this. He'll probably break my heart. What if he's married? Something is taking him away for long periods of time. He has to be married."

"Jeanine," Giselle blurted, as she got out of her car and greeted Grants sister on the porch. "GiGi," Jeanine said, as she hugged her. "Jeanine turned and walked in the house as Giselle followed her. She looked at Grant and smiled and he smiled back at her, desiring her but keeping his cool. The women sat on the couch and talked while Grant and Daniel drank beers and talked about past games and prominent figures in sports.

"So GiGi. What happened with you and Grant," Jeanine asked, in a low voice so that the men, who were in the other room, wouldn't hear. Giselle shook her head. "I don't know Jeanine. I love him but I'm not in love. I have fallen in love with someone else. We just grew apart," she stated, looking directly in Jeanine's eyes hoping she understood. Giselle wasn't ready to disclose all the details about her and Alonzo. Even though her and Jeanine were friends that was still Grants sister. Anything she told Jeanine she might as well tell Grant so she stayed vague with her explanation. But Jeanine understood. She believed a person should follow their heart. She didn't believe in staying with someone out of obligation. She believed in love. She was lucky enough to be in love with her husband. She didn't fault Giselle for how she felt and respected that she was honest with Grant. "At least he knows. It's good you told him Gi," she replied. Time had passed and Grant and Daniel walked in the room and announced they were ready to go. Jeanine pleaded with Giselle to go with them but she repeatedly turned her down. She said she was tired and had to go. After several more minutes of talking, Giselle left and Grant, Daniel and Jeanine left for *Sizzle's Restaurant* in town.

Chapter Twelve - Mated

Giselle pulled up and looked around. She sighed then got out of her car and went into her home. She sat her keys down and then held her forehead. She had a headache coming on and went to her medicine cabinet to find something to take. *Oh no. Is this it,* she said, as she shook the almost empty bottle of Tylenol. She was stressing about Alonzo and had given herself a mild headache. She took the top off and one pill came tumbling out. She looked at it and then popped it in her mouth. She swallowed a small Dixie cup of water and then looked at herself in the mirror. *Get it together Giselle!*

Just as she started to get emotional about him again, he appeared at her sliding door. "Alonzo," she said, as she opened the door. Giselle's headache seemed to disappear as fast as it started. Alonzo walked in and kissed her then bluntly asked her where she had been. "Where were you Giselle," he asked. Giselle was caught off guard. She was prepared to ask him that. He was the one who had disappeared that morning and then stayed away all day. But she was glad to see him and so she would tell him anything he wanted to hear. She was glad he asked. She liked that he asked. It showed concern and maybe a bit of jealousy. "I went to see Grant's sister," she said.

Alonzo stared at her. He looked away then asked her what he really wanted to know. He had been channeling her thoughts but he wouldn't hear everything if something was blocking what she was thinking. He wouldn't hear everything if she was in love or falling in love with another man. He would lose the ability and not even know until it was too late. "Are you still seeing him? Do you love him?" he asked. Giselle looked down and shook her head. She was somewhat disappointed in the question. She looked at him but said nothing at first. She thought for sure he could tell. She thought for certain that her body language and the fact that she was out of control with him was apparent. "No! I'm not seeing him. I don't love him. I'm in love with you. Can't you see it. Don't you feel it. Why would you question anything at this point when you have me totally," she said, still shaking her head in disbelief. "But I don't know about you. You leave all the time. You stay away. You wouldn't make love to me. I don't know what I've gotten myself into here," she said, as she went on and on exposing her feelings and being open and honest with him.

Giselle stopped mid-sentence when she noticed Alonzo's eyes change. His gaze changed and he was now standing in front of her with a blank expression. Alonzo didn't hear anything after the words *I love you*. His body shut down on him and although he was still standing in front of her looking at her his mind was elsewhere. The curse had lifted and the cells in his body had started to change. Every cell in his body went through rapid changes and Giselle started panicking. "What's wrong," she said, getting closer in his face. There was something empty in his gaze and Giselle panicked.

She noticed he wasn't reacting to anything she said and so she grabbed his face. He was hot to the touch. "Alonzo what's wrong?" she asked. After a few minutes of silence, she shook him. "Alonzo… Say something. What is it? Are you sick? Why are you so hot? Talk to me baby?" she pleaded, growing concerned as her own face filled with fear. After a few moments of intense hot flashes Alonzo's head cleared. He closed his eyes and then opened them and looked at Giselle. She smiled. He was back. He seemed more intense. Alonzo kissed her.

"What happened?" Giselle asked, feeling his head and believing he had fallen ill right before her eyes. "Nothing," he said, as he grabbed her and kissed her then carried her up the stairs to her room. "Oh my gosh baby. You scared the shit out of me. You're staying with me this time. Why do you keep leaving? Where do you go?" she asked, as she held onto him with her legs wrapped around his waist. "To make things right, so I can spend the rest of my life with you. I love you too. I'm not going anywhere Giselle," Alonzo replied. "Good… Then you can go. I trust you. Completely," Giselle said, as she laid her head on his shoulder.

Alonzo let Giselle down easy and held her face, kissing her intensely as she grabbed him tight. She noticed he wasn't radiating heat like before. Giselle loved his kisses. They were passionate and filled with love and there was an intense energy behind each one. Something she'd never felt. She grabbed his penis and stroked it. She wanted to make sure that it would be hers this night. "You are not leaving here without giving me this," she said. Alonzo laughed. "What!" he said. "You heard me," she said, as she kissed him. Giselle backed up and sat on the edge of her bed. "Come here," she said. Alonzo was the epitome of sexy and Giselle was ready. He pulled his shirt over his head revealing the body she had dreamed about. He walked to her and she grabbed him and pulled him to the bed. He was taking too long to get to her.

Giselle unzipped his pants then unbuttoned them and pulled them down to his knees. "Damn. Ok. Um. Alonzo this is a bit much but I am determined baby," she said, as she put the tip of his dick in her mouth. Alonzo closed his eyes and moaned. Her mouth felt warmer than his body and he was ready to implode and fill it with all that his body carried. Giselle took her time. He was more than she thought she could handle but managed to take it like a pro. She grabbed his ass and guided him in her mouth as far as she could take him. Which wasn't far at all. But it was enough for Alonzo. He moaned and held her head as he tried not to come. He had never been inside a woman's mouth. He had not been inside a woman and so he planned for a long night.

Grant and his family left the restaurant and walked to the car. Grant was stopped for a brief moment by a concerned citizen about a complaint she had regarding noisy neighbors. Grant instructed her on how to file an official complaint then got in the car and drove back home. It was a cool and dark night and the streets were lit by the full moon in the sky. Grant noticed the moon and there was something about the night that seemed eerie. He drove down the main round and turned off on his street as he looked around. He wasn't sure why he felt so uneasy. He was sure it was just jitters. Jeanine and her husband laughed and talked about the family that sat behind them. How they had sent every plate back to either be re-cooked or changed. They laughed at how the waiter was annoyed to the point of being obvious.

Grants phone rang and he looked at the caller id. He didn't recognize the number but took the call anyway. It was after hours and work-related things were usually radioed to him using the issued radios. "Hello," he said. "Sheriff Ellis this is Vince Stiegel from the lab," he replied. "Yes. Yes. What you got," he asked. "Well, it's all very confusing. The DNA we tested was neither human or animal but a combination of both. There are similarities within DNA with man versus other animals, but this was unlike anything we've seen. It took me this long to get back to you because we ran the test multiple times and we came back to the same conclusion. My colleagues say the findings are impossible. They are have determined that the results are inconclusive," he advised. Grant held the phone. This is what Chitto was trying to say but never truly would say. Grant now believed the legend he originally heard and deemed old wives tales as true. "Thanks Vince," he said, as he hung up. Grant was in a daze. He was speechless.

Grant listened and laughed at his family as they joked around. He tried to engage with them but was too distracted to weigh in on their conversation. He looked around as he drove up his driveway, still uneasy and now with knots in his stomach. He had been uneasy the entire ride home. He had recently seen paw prints in the sandy dirt near his car and wondered what had left them. But that wasn't unusual. What was unusual was the size. They were large like a bears paw. "Be careful when you get out the car. I thought I saw bears paws," he warned. "Where's your gun?" his sister asked. "I have it. But still. Be careful," he said.

Grant, his sister and her husband exited the car. Jeanine was still laughing and talking with her husband and the two hadn't paid attention to their surroundings. Grant was on alert. He looked around, paying close attention to the bushes. As the trio started to walk, a large grey and white wolf leaped from behind a bush. The wolf grabbed Daniel and tossed him around like a rag doll, as Grant and

Jeanine watched in horror. Jeanine screamed and Grant opened the car door and pushed her inside then reached for his gun and shot the wolf. The wolf was undeterred and turned towards him and started approaching him slowly. "Grant!" Jeanine shouted. Jeanine climbed to the other side of the car and looked on the ground then screamed when she saw her husbands mutilated body lying there. "Stay in the car Jeanine!" Grant said, as he aimed the gun at the wolfs head.

Alonzo was holding Giselle and kissing her on the top of her head as she slept on his chest. He became alarmed and his senses picked up fear. He smelled human blood in the air. He eased from under Giselle and got out of bed. He rushed to put his clothes on then stood at her balcony's sliding door. His senses picked up on something amidst and close by. He could feel the heightened level of fear and a strong smell of blood in the air. He knew that Darius was attacking a human and looked back at Giselle, who was still sleeping. Alonzo exited then jumped over her railing. He ran through the brush and vegetation, towards the attack. He could hear screams. He could sense fear and pain. Alonzo turned into Blackwolf and ran in the direction of the smell of blood. Unaware that he was going to end up at Grants home.

Giselle was dreaming of something pleasant when her dream suddenly shifted. The scene involved the same black wolf. The wolf that she wondered about. The one that had interjected itself in her life and that she looked at as a pet. And was in her dreams. The scene was hard to visualize. She couldn't see things clearly. But Giselle had a sense of danger and death. After a few minutes the attack came into focus. She could see him attacking and savagely destroying another wolf of similar size. Giselle stood by and watched as the black wolf ripped the other wolf's head off which caused her to jolt awake. "What is with my dreams?" she said, as she held her head, and tried to catch her breath.

She looked over to Alonzo's side of the bed and saw that he was not there. Giselle stared into the darkness and had a flash of the black wolf in a fight and then saw the silhouette of a man that appeared to be Grant. "Ok. I'm not sleep. Or am I. Why am I seeing things?" she said, as she looked around.

Giselle called out to Alonzo to make sure he was not in the house then got up and put her clothes on. "I'm going to Grants. Somethings not right. That dream meant something. I have to go see," she said, as he got dressed, grabbed her keys and headed out the door.

Darius slowed his walk toward Grant when he aimed the gun at his head. The bullet would not kill him but metal slowed shifter wolves down. Any metal. And silver was fatal. Grant was surprised at the size of the wolf. He was shocked that this wolf was not the black one that was at Giselle's house. He backed away slowly as he looked around. Darius continued approaching him and Grant fired three shots which stunned Darius but did not stop him. Grant decided to try to run for a tree and when he turned around, Darius grabbed him and tossed him ten feet into the air. Just as Darius braced for his attack, Giselle pulled up and gasped at the sight before her. She put her hands over her face. She couldn't bear to watch the animal attack Grant. Giselle grabbed her phone and called for help. "Hello. This is Giselle Jackson. Grant is in trouble. He's being attacked by a wolf," she yelled. The deputy told her they were on their way and Giselle hung up. "Where's your gun Grant. Shoot it," she said.

Grant had landed on the hood of his car and held his arm as the pain from the break took hold. Jeanine screamed out and then looked over and saw Giselle was sitting in her car not too far away. Grant moaned as Darius walked toward the car, growling and savoring the moment. Just as he got close to the car and raised his body up to crawl on top of the car, Alonzo leaped out from the vegetation and snatched Darius by his neck and swung him into a tree. Darius' hind legs hit the tree and he came running toward Alonzo. He tried to bite Alonzo but was grabbed again, this time by the shoulder and Alonzo tore a huge chunk out of his flesh, seriously wounding Darius.

Alonzo circled Darius. This was the end. He would deal with Darius' brutal and cruel behavior any longer. He saw his plan clearly. The plan was to set him and his pack up and now his pack was dead. Blackwolf growled as his anger made way to a violent series of thoughts. Because there was another plan to kill Giselle and for that, he would have to die. Grant eased down off the hood. It was obvious to him, that the black wolf had just saved him. The animal he originally hunted was now the protector. Blackwolf growled a loud and menacing growl then leaped and ferociously attacked Darius, tossing him around like a rag doll. He bit into his back and shoulders, removing large chunks of flesh as Darius whimpered and tried to fight back. Alonzo threw Darius against a tree stump then growled as he approached him. He tortured him. He prolonged his death. Darius was evil and had caused him great pain. And so there would be no quick death. Darius, bleeding and injured but still able to fight, braced for another attacked as he tried to defend himself. Alonzo viciously bit chunks of flesh from Darius body until he was no longer moving. As a final act of savageness, Blackwolf grabbed him by the throat and ripped his throat from his body as he tossed him towards the trees. Grant held his arm and yelled out in pain when he tried to move it. His arm was broken in two spots.

Alonzo walked over to the car and looked Grant in the eyes. For a moment he thought about killing him. He believed Grant had killed his wolf family and he wanted revenge. Grant, still on the ground, held his hand up as a gesture of peace and Alonzo relented. As he began to walk away, Alonzo looked out into the road and saw Giselle sitting in her car horrified. She locked eyes with Blackwolf. She gasped as she realized who it was. She sat there in shock. She knew it was Alonzo and was in disbelief. It was the same wolf that had befriended her and she now recognized him. The same wolf from when she was ten years old. Her connection to him was strong. She realized the visions she had was through his eyes. From his vantage point. But her analytical mind would not let her believe the conclusion she had drawn. That couldn't be him. How could a man be a wolf? It didn't make sense. But the eyes. The look. It was him

Giselle thought of the visit she made to Chitto and what he had told her. She was not aware that Alonzo had channeled her spirit completely. But she now understood what Chitto meant by marked. She understood that she was channeled. That it was him all along tapping into her physically through a mental connection. He was the source of her orgasms. It was all so clear. And now she could see things she would not have been able to see or sense before. Giselle's breathing slowed and she thought she heard voices in her head. She tried to tune into what was being said and clearly heard Alonzo's voice and could read his thoughts. Giselle became terrified at first. *Am I losing my mind*, she thought. Giselle looked back at the wolf then had a moment of clarity. She could feel his spirit and she knew exactly who he was.

Alonzo locked thoughts with Giselle. He knew that Giselle was now aware that it was him. Alonzo stared at her for a moment. His angry thoughts had calmed. He felt calm in her presence. He turned his attention back to Grant. He had plans on telling her one day and so he felt a weight had been lifted. It was ok if she saw him clearly. She was to be his wife and the mother of his kids and she would need to know in case they had a son.

He stared at Grant and Grant stared back. Grant stood up and limped slowly to his shed. He emerged after a few moments with a large metal cage. He sat it on the ground and raised the door. To Alonzo's surprise, three small wolf pups came out. The wolf pups immediately went to Alonzo and he looked at Grant and then smelled the pups. Alonzo looked at Giselle, then disappeared into the woods as the pups followed. Grant felt good about giving the pups back. He had got them from Steve Mitchell's brothers who went into the woods to shoot the wolves after Steve was killed. He hoped that giving them back would make amends to a wolf that had just saved his life.

Giselle waited for Alonzo every day, looking for him to emerge from the forest. It had been two weeks since he had disappeared into the trees with the pups and she eagerly anticipated his return. Each day brought worry and sadness as she began to miss him terribly but she knew he would be returning. He always returned to her. She knew that Grant and his men would not be hunting the animals any longer. Grant vowed to get funding to invest in opening a sanctuary so he could protect rather than destroy, the states wildlife.

Giselle watched the trees sway in the wind as she sipped her tea. Her morning ritual that had been her mainstay to calm and relax her mind. It had been long enough and she was now missing Alonzo more than ever. "Come home baby. I miss you," she whispered, hoping that he could hear her and feel her energy. As she turned to go in the kitchen, a warm and euphoric feeling came over her. Giselle smiled. "He heard me," she said, as she closed her eyes. She was afraid to turn around and be disappointed but she knew that felling. It was undeniable. Giselle looked back and saw him emerge from the forest. He smiled when he saw her in the window. He could see her excitement as he walked towards her. Giselle sat her cup down and opened her door. She ran to him and jumped on him, wrapping her legs around him. "Oh baby. I missed you.," she said, as she kissed him fervently. "I missed you too," he said, smiling and happy to be back. "How are they doing?" she asked, concerned about the pups. The only survivors from his pack. "Good. They have a new family now," he said. Alonzo carried Giselle into the house and they didn't emerge until a week later.

"Good morning Giselle," Beth said, as the two smiled at one another. Beth and Jason were going strong and Giselle and Alonzo were inseparable. It had been a year since the fateful night that changed the course of history. Grant was now

Mayor and had approved a sanctuary to protect and preserve wildlife. With funding from Giselle and her soon to be husband Alonzo, the sanctuary had a start. Soon, funding poured in from outraged citizens who found out about the wolf massacre and wanted something done about it. Giselle was donating her time to the sanctuary and Alonzo went there often to visit the three pups. He had placed them there until he could come up with a plan to get them in the wild. The pups were being raised by a female alpha wolf that was now living in the sanctuary. The wolves were tagged and monitored in the wild which comprised of a ten mile area.

Giselle was sitting in her office when Mr. Garner walked in. "Yes," she said, as he approached her desk. "I just wanted to tell you that you did a great job on the Swanson account. They were very happy with what you came up with and are signing off on the final design," he said. Giselle smiled. "Oh well that's great to hear," she said. "And I have a new client that I want you to meet. We are going to do a presentation with them. So, mark your calendar," he said, smiling as he left out. He was glad to have Giselle back. He noticed she was happy and her work was better than ever.

Giselle crossed her legs and pulled her chair closer to the desk. She typed in the name of her client and waited for her computer to pull up their account. Giselle glanced out the window and looked to the sky. It was crystal clear. Not a single cloud. Why is this thing so slow right now," she said, as the computer seemed to stall. She glanced at her phone then back to the computer. Alonzo would be calling her soon. He had mentioned meeting her for lunch but they didn't make it a definite plan. "Oh Giselle. I wanted to show you something Cyber found. I'm thinking of investing in this company's templates," Mr. Garner said, as he walked back in her office. He sat his laptop down in front of her and began to show her new design templated for first pages and landing pages.

"Wow. These are creative. I like these," Giselle said, as she flipped through them. Giselle rubbed her neck. Her body slowly became warm. She began to feel hot and tense and started moving around in her chair. She tried to keep a straight face as her vagina had a mind of its own and began throbbing and pulsating. Giselle wanted Mr. Garner to hurry and say whatever he needed to say. Then leave before he witnessed something he shouldn't. "You ok Giselle," Mr. Garner asked. "Oh Yes. I'm ok. My back itches," she replied, as she braced for a powerful and earth-shattering orgasm. She stood up and went to her window and smiled at Alonzo as he stood in his favorite spot, leaning against the wall of a small building.

"I'm going to kill you. Just wait," she quietly mouthed, as she shook her head at him, smiling. She knew he could see her clearly. Alonzo smiled and walked toward the coffee shop. "Giselle," Mr. Garner said, as he stood there. When she didn't respond he grabbed his laptop and walked out, shaking his head. Mr. Garner walked up to Beth. "You notice anything weird about Giselle," he asked. "Yes. All the time. I notice it all the time," she said, smiling.

Please leave a <u>Review</u>! If you purchased the paperback, please log into your account and leave feedback. It is appreciated!

Thank you!

Make sure to check out my other books!

Smokey Moment

More Books By

Smokey Moment

Standalones

The Twin

He Came To Me

French Kissed

Everything I Want

Secrets, Lies & Video

Keeping Him Quiet

Pretty Fin

Gifted

Through The Wires

Beauty is Sleeping

Baby Girl

I Am Her

Two-part Sagas, Series or Trilogies:

Ways of Kings I

Ways of Kings II

Stray I

Stray II New Life

Stray III Covenant

Rocks and Stones Between a Rose Part I

Rocks and Stones Between a Rose Part II

BookBabe

For information on use of this material or for help with indie publishing needs contact Smokey Moment.

Email us at: bookbabepublishing@gmail.com

Thank you!

Smokey Moment

Appt Confirmation: 80475386
11³⁰ NOV 2ⁿᵈ

AWA
SAG
B191 PIN

F7P08G (D. Conf.)

Made in the USA
Middletown, DE
24 October 2020

21988175R00177